Who Killed

The death of a

and other short stories
by Gary Comenas

Jackleton Press, London, 2023

Note: No text in this book was created with A.I.

*When I get nervous
I tell the truth*

Contents

Who Killed Wonderboy? 3

Morocco 51

Selma Avenue 88

Nick 95

Blanche 112

Who Killed Wonderboy?

Eric Emerson:

I'm not a male superstar, I'm a, I feel more like a 'wonderboy' because I don't want to be a superstar like everyone else. I don't consider myself part of the Warhol crowd, I don't hang around with them... I don't associate with them... I just come to do my thing... I have my own things going... I have my musical group and I wanna, you know, work on that rather than become a Warhol superstar. (*Andy Makes a Movie*, Dir: Robert Emmet Smith, 1968)

* * *

When I began researching the lives of Andy Warhol's superstars for a website I was creating, it wasn't Eric Emerson's life that interested me; it was his death. Although he had the good looks of a Warhol star - with his shoulder-length blond hair and youthful ballet-trained body, there was something missing. He seemed too full of himself on-screen, too much of a show-off. He lacked the casual charm of superstars like Joe Dallesandro (who appeared with Eric in *Lonesome*

Cowboys and *Heat*) or the stoned charisma of the hippie-in-y-fronts, Patrick Fleming, from *The Chelsea Girls* (which also included Eric in the cast). When Eric complained about "not wanting to be a superstar like everyone else" in the above quote, it wasn't because he wanted to be accepted as an ordinary guy, but because he considered himself as something greater than a superstar - a "wonderboy." I wondered if his hubris had played a part in his demise.

The main problem with trying to figure out what caused Eric's death was that there were so many different versions of it. Some sources said he was the victim of a 'hit and run' driver; others said it was a heroin overdose that killed him. At least a couple of his friends claimed it was "murder." I couldn't figure out if his colleagues were trying to protect the memory of their friend or trying to protect themselves.

The generally accepted version of his death was the one that appeared in *Popism, the Warhol 60s* by Andy Warhol and Pat Hackett:

> *They found Eric Emerson one early morning in the middle of Hudson Street. Officially, he was labelled a hit-and-run victim, but we heard rumours that he'd overdosed and just been dumped there - in any case, the bicycle*

he'd been riding was intact.[1]

The explanation covered most possibilities by using the word "rumours," but no sources were given for the rumours.

I needed to know more. I began by comparing the different accounts of what happened to the one that appeared in *Popism*. There were holes in all of them.

* * *

The account in *Popism* that claimed that Eric's bicycle was "intact" contradicted what Warhol's scriptwriter, Ron Tavel, wrote about Eric's death. In Tavel's version, Eric's bicycle was "broken" and thrown beside his body in the street to "simulate a traffic accent."

Ron referred to the death in an introduction to the scenario he wrote for a Warhol film he refers to as *Jail*, filmed in 1967. He wrote the introduction much later, after Eric's death:

> *In May 1975 he [Eric] either O'D' ed on heroin or was murdered, his body carelessly tossed into the street and his bicycle broken and thrown beside it to simulate a traffic*

---

[1] Andy Warhol and Pat Hackett, *Popism: The Warhol Sixties* (NY: Harcourt Brace, 1980), p. 299.

> *accident. Couldn't have fooled a rookie nark,*
> *but there was no investigation.*

Tavel's comment that "There was no investigation," is particularly noteworthy. If Eric had been the subject of a hit and run, his death would have been investigated by the police to find out who the driver of the car was who hit him. But an overdose? There were so many of them in New York that it's doubtful that more than a cursory investigation would have taken place, if at all. In 1975, the year of Eric's death, Selwyn Raab wrote in the *New York York Times*:

> *New York is experiencing its worst illegal narcotics trafficking problems in five years, according to high law enforcement officials... heroin overdose deaths apparently are rising this year - a grim sign that the addict population may be increasing...*
>
> *Police officials project more than 1000 overdose deaths year... This steep rise may be attributed partly to an increase in addicts and partly to the availability of stronger heroin.*[2]

---

[2] Selwyn Raab, "Illegal Narcotics Traffic Is Worst Here in 5 Years," *The New York Times*, 8 December 1975, p.1 col. 2.

Eric may have been a superstar to Warhol fans but to the police he was just another statistic.

Murder would have been a different story, of course, but I wondered what Tavel meant when he suggested that Eric *"was murdered."* Did he mean an actual, premeditated murder or was he using the term figuratively? Murdered by whom? And why?

Had the cause of Eric's death become confused by the different versions of it that appeared over the years? *Popism* was published in 1980, five years after his death. I went back to the beginning and looked at how his ex-partners described his death just days after it happened.

* * *

Eric died on 28 May 1975. Reporters from the *New York Post* met up with two of his ex-partners less than a week later - their article came out in the June 4th issue of the *Post*. The women they interviewed were Jane Forth and Barbara Winter.

Forth had starred in *Trash* (produced by Andy Warhol, directed by Paul Morrissey) and was the mother of one of Eric's children, Emerson Forth - now the owner of a tattooing business in Florida who has also had small roles in several Hollywood films, including *Bad Boys II* (2003), *Vandal* (2019) and *Joey* (1986).

The other woman, Barbara Winter, was Eric's girlfriend at the time of his death. She was also the ex-wife (and sometimes referred to as the ex-manager) of the rock singer Edgar Winter. The debut album of the Edgar Winter Group, *They Only Come Out at Night*, was released in November 1972 and reached no. 3 on the Billboard 200 chart. It stayed in the chart for 80 weeks. Barbara had a writing credit on one of the songs which meant she qualified for royalties. She was also rumoured to have received a generous alimony settlement when Edgar and she divorced. She started seeing Eric in late 1973. Edgar married another woman in 1979.

The *New York Post* article was the first version of Eric's death to appear in print in a mainstream newspaper and it differed considerably from the *Popism* account which appeared five years later.

The *Post* reporters wrote:

> *[Eric] Emerson's time ended last Wednesday. He was hit by a car and killed while crossing the street somewhere between his apartment at 80 North Moore St. and the Market Diner at West and Laight Sts.*
>
> *Friends said it happened shortly after he had returned from a party at the Fashion*

> *Institute of Technology. Police said the time of the accident was 3 p.m.*[3]

But if Eric's body was found "one early morning" (according to *Popism*), it must have gone unnoticed for a considerable time if the accident occurred at 3 pm (according to the *New York Post*). Maybe one of the sources mixed up their a.m.'s with their p.m.'s but there was another conspicuous difference. No bicycle is mentioned in the *Post* article. Also, no other accounts mention a party at F.I.T. Did the *Post* get that information from Barbara or Jane? It's unclear from the article whether Eric went back to his (and Barbara's) apartment after the alleged party and then left again before getting "hit by a car."

Another description of Eric's death appeared in the autobiography *Famous for 15 Minutes: My Years with Andy Warhol* by the Warhol superstar, Ultraviolet, published in 1988:

> *Eric Emerson, the pretty, psychedelic playboy who liked both pretty boys and pretty girls and fathered four children, was found dead near the West Side Highway*

---

[3] Mel Juffee and Peter Keepnews, "He Brought 'Glitter to Rock Music," *New York Post*, 4 June 1975, p. 46. Reproduced at: http://www.magictramps.com/pages/memory.htm.

> *early one morning in May 1975; he lay next to his bicycle, which was found unscratched.*

The West Side Highway was near North Moore and Laight Street where Eric and Barbara's apartment was. Unlike the *Post*, Ultraviolet does mention a bicycle which she says was "unscratched," similar to the claim made in *Popism* that it was "intact." Ultra doesn't give a source for her information and, unlike Jane and Barbara, wasn't particularly close to Eric.

A year after Ultra's book came out, David Bourdon published his biography of Andy Warhol which gave the following account of Eric's death. He also mentioned the "unscratched" bicycle:

> *In May 1975, Eric Emerson, the scintillating star of [The] Chelsea Girls, Lonesome Cowboys, and a thousand shenanigans in the back room of Max's Kansas City, was found dead at age thirty-one near the West Side Highway, apparently the victim of a hit-and-run driver.*
>
> *Eric (who for a period in the early 1970s, had lived with Jane Forth and fathered a son by her) was known as a reckless bicycle rider who paid little attention to traffic as he sped,*

> *yodelling, through the canyons of Manhattan.*
>
> *But the bicycle alongside his body was unscratched, leading friends to suspect that perhaps he had overdosed elsewhere and had been deposited in the street to simulate an accident.*[4]

David didn't say who his sources were, but, in general, his book - simply titled *Warhol* - is probably the most accurate reader-friendly biography of the artist. Bourdon was part of the New York art scene in the sixties and wrote a column for the *Village Voice*. He knew Warhol and travelled with him to Arizona when the Pop artist filmed his western *Lonesome Cowboys* there which included Eric in the cast.

I assumed that Bourdon's version of Eric's death was a mixture of what appeared in *Popism* and the gossip of the day. Although I had quoted the *Popism* version on my website, the lack of a conclusive cause of death continued to bother me. Then I was contacted by a woman named Krysteen Walraven - and that changed everything.

* * *

---

[4] David Bourdon, *Warhol* (NY: Harry N. Abrams Inc., 1989), p. 347.

Krysteen has never appeared in any Warhol biographies or books about the Factory. Her only connection to the Warhol scene was her relationship with Eric (she was the mother to another of his children - Monique) and her appearance in a Cecil Beaton photograph of the Factory crowd that I had on my website. Previously, she had been captioned as "unidentified" whenever the photograph was published.

Soon after we started corresponding, Krysteen wrote:

> *Gary, I just looked at your Factory site and you have a picture of me on it - the first page where we are all standing around Andy at a table. I am standing next to Eric. Love Krysteen.* [5]

Later she explained why she looked so miserable in the photograph:

> *I was pregnant you know, but Eric, he was always trying to think of ways to get money for us... You can see I don't look very happy.*

---

[5] Email from Krysteen, Saturday, August 10, 2002, at 07:31 PM.

> *It was because of the movie idea. Eric wanted Andy to do this movie, and in that movie, he wanted me to give birth…*
>
> *I was glad when Andy said he was not ready to do live birth. It would be too unappealing. I think that was how he put it…*

Surprisingly, in regard to the photograph, Krysteen didn't know who Cecil Beaton was. When I told her, she asked, "Is Cecil Beaton still alive? I would like to see the rest of the pictures because he did trippy ones in the mirror with me and Andy hiding in the shot. I have never seen that one…"

Then she gave her opinion on Andy Warhol:

> *Andy, I did not like because he made Eric beg for his money. And when we needed it so bad. I thought Andy owed more than he ever gave.*
>
> *Eric went to work at Max's as the Maître d' to earn money… he also slept around like a gigolo to get money.*

And finally, she told me why she thought Eric's

death wasn't accidental:

> *Eric had a mean side to him and the way I watched him verbally abuse different people when he did not get his way... He did that to the wrong person and that's why I don't think the death was accidental.*
>
> *He also used to use force on different people; anything to get his way...*[6]

Had somebody murdered Eric out of revenge? I'd learn more later when Krys connected with Eric's birth family at a family reunion.

Krysteen and I ended up writing to each other for several years as she took me on a tour of the swinging sixties and beyond; what it was really like from the perspective of someone who just hung out during that era - who wasn't after underground fame. She had nothing to risk by being truthful with me because her means of support didn't depend on having a Warhol connection.

Her tales about hanging out in Hollywood during the sixties reminded me of what it was like when I hung out there the following decade. I was familiar with at least

---

[6] Krysteen, 12 August 2002 at 22:22:02 BST.

some of the places she mentioned - certainly the Whiskey which is where she met Eric. According to Krys, he was hanging out in L.A. after filming *Lonesome Cowboys* in nearby Arizona. I wondered if she was confusing *Lonesome Cowboys* with *San Diego Surf* which was filmed in La Jolla.

"It was just before my (18th) birthday," she recalled when she met Eric outside the Whiskey. "He told me he was going to to make me everything he wanted in a woman..."[7]

Everything *he* wanted. What about her needs? I asked what this "wonderboy's" secret was. *Why* was he so popular? Krys explained that, in addition to having a good "sense of humour," Eric was "well endowed..."

"I think he could have made a dog happy," Krys said. "Eric fucked anything that moved, male or female and there were so many of them... he gave me clap five times."[8]

When Eric left L.A. to return to New York, Krys followed, already pregnant with her and Eric's daughter. She initially lived with Eric at Elda Gentile's apartment. Elda would give birth to another of Eric's children, Branch Emerson, the following year on 14 December 1970. (Krys and Eric's daughter, Monique was born on 17 July 1969.)

---

[7] Krysteen, 12 June 2003 06:08.
[8] Krysteen, 12 June 2003 06:08.

Elda was the founder of a band called The Stilettos, with Debbie Harry on vocals. Elda's previous band was Pure Garbage with Andy Warhol's drag star superstar, Holly Woodlawn, on vocals.[9]

In New York, Krys and Eric hung out at Max's Kansas City where Eric was already known as a part of the Warhol crowd. According to Krys, he would have sex with other women in the men's bathroom or "over by the telephone..."

The women he had sex with at Max's included Debbie Harry who worked there during her pre-Blondie days. "I made it with Eric in a phone booth upstairs," Debbie later recalled. "One time only."[10]

Life with Eric and Elda was fraught with complications as each of the women thought they were Eric's favourite. According to Krys, Elda was "madly in love with Eric" but that "he only used her for the money and a place to stay."

Elda apparently attacked Krysteen (and her unborn child) at one point. Krys said that Holly Woodlawn saved her life and asked if I could get a message of

---

[9] Holly starred in *Trash* - usually advertised as *Andy Warhol's Trash* but directed by his colleague Paul Morrissey. She was also the Holly in Lou Reed's song *Walk on the Wild Side*: "Holly came from Miami, F.L.A./Hitch-hiked her way across the U.S.A./ Plucked her eyebrows on the way/Shaved her legs and then he was a she/She says, "Hey, babe/Take a walk on the wild side...."
[10] Dick Porter and Chris Needs, *Parallel Lives Blondie* (London: Omnibus Press), Chapter 2 Village Heads. (Kindle)

thanks to her, which I did.

To Holly, Krys wrote:

> *Hello Holly, you might not remember me, but you saved mine and my baby's life one night in N.Y., lower east side apt at Elda's place.*
>
> *Eric and I were staying there and she [Elda] went off trying to cut my baby from my belly. You picked me up and took me to Pepper's apt.*
>
> *My name is Krysteen and my daughter Monique... is also Eric's daughter... I left N.Y in Nov. 69 to raise her somewhat normal, and around family.*
>
> *Anyway i [sic] never did get to thank you for carrying me downstairs to Ron and Peppers to keep Elda away from me, so I am now doing that.*
>
> *I wish you only the best things in this life. You gave me a chance to keep my baby safe*

and she has been all my happiness.[11]

"Pepper," mentioned in Krys' email, was Pepper Davis, one of the actresses in *The Chelsea Girls*. With her Southern accent and dressed like a farmer's daughter, she seemed out of place in that film with its flagrant scenes of shooting up and S & M flavoured violence. She looked confused and slightly frightened, as if she didn't understand what was going on. She probably didn't. Her pupils were the size of pins - usually a sign of heroin use. She wasn't as innocent as she looked. Krysteen later told me that they posed together for a feature in the porn magazine, *Screw*, and Eric wasn't very happy when he found out.

* * *

After a brief stay with Pepper and Ron, Krys joined Eric in an apartment on the Bowery where he was staying with friends. They lived together until Monique was born and then Eric moved "down the street." He was doing "too much dope" and Krysteen didn't want it near the baby. By "dope," Krys meant heroin.

Krysteen wrote:

---

[11] Email from Krysteen, 3 August 2002 22:02:45.

> ... I felt too much dope for a baby was bad.
> So, Eric stayed down the street. And he
> would come by everyday. And when I had
> someone to watch Monique we would go out.
>
> Eric started to do a lot of heroin and was not
> doing so well just before I left.
>
> He got to the point where he would come by
> and stand down in the street yelling up to
> my apartment begging for five bucks for a
> nickel bag.[12]

A nickel bag was $5.00 worth of heroin. Eric wasn't the only person doing junk at the time. Debbie Harry also indulged, later recalling "I was a junkie; everyone was a junkie."[13]

Krys left New York when Eric started arguing that Monique, their daughter, should be with both of them:

> ... one day, after Eric came by in very bad
> shape, because he was drinking a lot also, we

---

[12] Krysteen, 3 September 2002, 22.41.

[13] Quoted in Dick Porter and Kris Needs, *Parallel Lives Blondie* (London: Omnibus Press, 2012), Chapter 2. (Kindle) Debbie also refers to her habit in Emine Saner, "Debbie Harry on heroin, rape, robbery – and why she still feels lucky," *The Guardian*, 1 October 2019.

> *got into an argument about Monique, and he said she should be with both of us.*
>
> *I got scared that he might come over and do something crazy so in the end of November [1969] I called my mother and asked for a plane ticket out of there fast.*
>
> *I told her what was going on and she not only got the plane ticket right away but had a cab sent to pick me up...*[14]

L.A. wasn't far enough from Eric for Krysteen, so she moved to Hawaii with Monique. They lived there until Monique's first birthday in July 1970.

***

Eric later returned to L.A. to pursue his musical career. A member of a band called Messiah, who had met Eric during the same visit when Eric met Krysteen, wrote to him in New York to see if he'd be interested in joining the band. Eric took him up on the offer and returned to Southern California around the time that Krys was trying to escape from him. After an earthquake

---

[14] Krys, 3 September 2002, 22:41.

in 1971, Eric convinced the band to move to New York where he thought he'd be able to get them gigs at Max's.

The first *Village Voice* ad for Messiah at Max's appears in a September 1971 issue of the *Voice*. They're billed as "Messiah with Eric Emerson." The ad shows Eric doing the splits in mid-air in the style of a *Grand Jeté* and listed performances on September 29th and 30th and Oct. 1st, 2nd and 3rd.[15]

Later *Voice* ads only mentioned Eric, although members of Messiah or, as they were later called, The Magic Tramps, were part of his backing band.

Eric may have thought he was working on his "musical group" as he refers to it in the quote at the beginning of this narrative, but the *Voice* reviewer likened him to a cabaret host. Richard Nusser wrote in the 9 December 1971 issue of the *Village Voice*, that Eric was "hosting a cabaret show upstairs at Max's these days."

The Magic Tramps received full billing when they played with Eric at the newly renovated Mercer Arts Center the following year (1972). It was during the Mercer period that Eric befriended Chris Stein who would later form Blondie with Deborah Harry. Chris noticed Eric when he opened for the New York Dolls at the Mercer:

---

[15] *Village Voice*, 30 September 1971.

> *I was in art school. I was at the School of Visual Arts, and I used to think that the [New York] Dolls were a drag act, so I never went to the see the Dolls.*
>
> *When I finally found out they were a rock band, I went to see them, and Eric was playing with them. He opened for them and I kind of liked him more.*
>
> *I got friendly with Eric and my last year at Visual Arts I got them to play at the school party.*[16]

Chris became Eric's roadie and "intermittent bass and guitar" player and Eric moved into Chris's apartment on First Avenue and First Street. It was Stein's first apartment; he had got it "like 1969 or 1970." Debbie Harry went to gigs at the Mercer where she eventually met Chris which led to a romance and the formation of Blondie.[17] The two never married and split up in 1985 but continued to work together.

---

[16] Yvonne Sewall-Ruskin, *High on Rebellion: Inside the Underground at Max's Kansas City* (NY: Open Road, 2016) Kindle ed.
[17] Dick Porter and Kris Needs, *Parallel Lives Blondie* (London: Omnibus Press, 2012) (Kindle)

By the time that Debbie met Chris, she was already singing in Elda's band, The Stilettos. She later recalled meeting Chris "when he [Chris] was a bass player for Eric Emerson. He would go down on his knees and everything; he was really different as a bass player than he is as a guitarist."[18]

When Chris and Debbie formed Blondie, they didn't include Eric, but they kept in touch with him. Debbie later admitted that she was one of the last people to see him alive. By that time, he had met his final girlfriend, Barbara Winter - one of the two women interviewed by the *Post* at the beginning of this story. They were both living in her high-rise on the Lower West Side, near the river when he died - presumably it was that apartment that Debbie Harry was referring to when she made a remark about seeing Eric the night of his death in the book *Making Tracks: The Rise of Blondie*:

> *One night we were over at Eric's apartment working on a tape of Heart of Glass on his TEAC four-track tape recorder, when he suddenly staggered out of the kitchen looking ashen. He looked even more*

---

[18] Dick Porter and Kris Needs, *Parallel Lives Blondie* (London: Omnibus Press, 2012) (Kindle).

distraught and sad when we left.

Being satisfied drove him crazy in the end, because he had everything, so he didn't care about anything anymore. He used to go out jogging every day and did feats of physical endurance like strapping twenty-pound weights on each ankle and then bicycling up to the Factory.

The next day we were sitting around the house just after we woke up when Barbara called with the bad news. 'Oh, Eric got hit by a truck.'

He had been a good friend and inspiration to so many people. We didn't quite understand what had happened, but we went up to a party/wake held for him and saw a lot of people from the earlier glitter days.[19]

When Harry described Eric as "ashen," was she describing his overdose that night? Not likely. That's not the way a heroin overdose happens. It's quicker. The person usually turns blue and then dies. If anything, her

---

[19] Debbie Harry, Chris Stein, Victor Bockris, *Making Tracks: The Rise of Blondie* (Boston, MA: Da Capo press, 1998), p. 31.

inclusion of the description shows that Eric was still alive before she left the apartment - an alibi which her later comment backs up - "We didn't quite understand what had happened."

She says that Barbara told her the next day that Eric was "hit by a truck." That was the first time I had heard about a truck. Debbie doesn't say Eric was on his bike, just that he rode his bike often. Why mention the "feats of physical endurance" at all?

It was unlikely that Eric was "bicycling up to the Factory" in 1975 because he didn't have any business there at the time; it was Warhol's third 'Factory' and usually just referred to as 'the office.' Eric's last film for Warhol - *Heat* - had been released in 1972.

Rather than having "everything" at that point in is life, as Debbie Harry described, Eric's life appeared to be falling apart. He wasn't appearing in Warhol films anymore; his musical career had ceased to take off; and he was addicted to smack. Presumably by "everything" Debbie was referring to the financial support Eric received from Barbara Winter which was assumed to come from the alimony she got from Edgar Winter.

Debbie says that Barbara rang the next day to tell them about Eric's death "just after we woke up." But how did Barbara find out so quickly the circumstances of his death? Who told her? If he had been hit by a truck, the police would have had to identify the body and arrange for it to be transported to a morgue. The first people they would have contacted would have been his family. Barbara and Eric were not married, and the officers who found the body on the side of the road (if that was what happened) would not have known that he was in a relationship with Barbara. How would they have determined a truck was responsible in such a short time? There were so many aspects of Barbara's story that didn't make sense.

Interestingly, Debbie Harry doesn't mention the night when Eric turned "ashen" in her later memoir, *Face It*. She mentions Eric, but mostly in passing. By the time *Face It* was published in 2019 (after the publication of *Making Tracks*), Eric had largely been written out of her life story.

* * *

Krysteen eventually made contact with Eric's family during our correspondence and got invited to the Emerson family reunion which took place around the date of Eric's death. It was there that she found out new information about his death that led her to believe he had been murdered.

Eric died on Wednesday, 28 May 1975 and Krys and Monique went to the reunion from the 23rd to the 27th of 2003. The Emersons were living in Tennessee by that time. They had previously lived in New Jersey where Eric was born and raised.

On 5 June 2003, about a week after Krys got back from the reunion, she wrote:

> *Things were going along just fine until... Eric's sister... started to take Monique around the house on a tour and asked me to come along.*
>
> *Eric's family believes in keeping lots of pictures and the walls were full of them. After about 3 rooms full of old pictures, I could not go on. I had to leave. It was all affecting me so much that I had to hold back the tears and run for the door. I got in my car and took off for anywhere but there...*
>
> *I started to remember stuff I forgot we ever did, people we partied with all the time, spent with the Beach Boys, Frank Zappa Joni Mitchell, Eric Clapton, just on and on and on. Memories came flooding back in like a broken dam.*

Krys had taken photographs of some of the pictures on the wall and sent them to me. There were quite a few of Eric as a child growing up in New Jersey and training to become a ballet dancer. One of the ballet pictures is on the cover of this book.

She also sent a picture of Eric in his school yearbook. On the upper left corner of his page his mother had written the following message:

> *Son -*
> *Hope you make it to the top and all your dreams come true.*
> *Love Mom*

Eric was greater than a superstar. He was a human being.

* * *

Only Krysteen and Elda were at the reunion from the New York days. Jane Forth and Barbara Winter - the two exes who gave the interview about Eric's death in the *New York Post* (the article mentioned earlier with the 'hit and run' explanation) - didn't attend.

I asked Krys if she had discussed Eric's death with Elda at the reunion. She told me what Elda had told her:

> *OK I will try to get it straight ... here goes.*
> *After trying to dodge Elda on the second day*

she followed me out to the car where I went to smoke. The whole thing was getting to me, and I started smoking again.

When she got there, I don't know what she expected of me - to just be nice and forget how awful she had been to me or what? So, when she started to say something to me, I stopped her and told her "You know Elda you were just awful to me, and you almost killed me. How could you do that to a preg. woman?"

Well, she shut up for a second and gathered her thoughts, then said..."Well Holly was there, and I knew that she would save you so I felt like I could do that."

I looked her straight in the eye and told her, "You owe me an apology" and she was quick to say, "I am sorry, could we forget that."

So, I said 'You know I was only 18 yrs. old, preg. far from home, and Eric is the one who brought me to your house to stay. I did not want to stay there but he said you were his friend."

So, Elda starts with "Branch [Elda's son by Eric] and Monique are bro. and sister they need each other - I am really very sorry Krysteen."

Then I asked, "Well then, Elda, what happened to Eric? I know he did not die the way they say he did."

She starts this big, long story about how much Eric really loved her and Branch even though he had another girlfriend - this Barbara.

It seems Jane [Forth] was pregnant again but not with his kid and she left him taking Emerson with her, so Eric gets this other girlfriend he had moved in with - Barbara - and was living with her.

Now Elda said at that time her band, The Stilettos, was trying to make it and Barbara was her agent or promoter something like that but all Barbara wanted to do was get Elda out of the picture, so Elda says.

> *She said this Barbara just wanted to promote her to get rid of her, but no way was she going to fall for that - she knew Eric wanted her and Branch and she says she talked Eric into making a loft in Barbara's place so Branch and her could visit Eric.*
>
> *Well, supposedly when Eric mentioned this to Barbara, she went wild, but Barbara had lots of $ and knew she could keep Eric with lots of dope [heroin]. So, when she finds out, she goes out and buys $300.00 worth of heroin and comes back and gives it to Eric.*
>
> *Now when this happens, she [Elda] swears that she was not there but there were 8 people in the apt at the time and then Elda looks at me and says he shot himself up with all the dope and nobody else put it in him - that he injected it all by himself.* [20]

Elda's description implicated Barbara as one of the eight people in the apartment at the time of Eric's overdose. But was Elda there? If not, how could she be so certain that Eric "injected it all by himself?"

---

[20] Krysteen, 10 June 2003 06:54

Krys thought that blaming Eric for his overdose was "bullshit:"

> *At this point I tell Elda "Bullshit. Eric never never had a death wish and he was well acquainted with how much dope he could do."*
>
> *I told her he would never do that because if she had done as much dope with him as I did, she knew how he used to check what he did before he did the stuff always. (You got to remember that he was the one that started shooting me up with dope for the first time and one of the things he taught me right off was how to test stuff first and not to trust anyone with the bag. He was always careful.)*
>
> *So, Elda says, 'well he did it to himself.' No one made him do it. Barbara just gave him enough to kill himself and that was her way of keeping Eric from seeing Branch and her. That Barbara was so jealous that she killed him rather than let him see Elda....*

It wasn't just Elda that Krysteen was angry about:

> *Do you believe that there were 8 people in the house [and] no one tried to help him? They were afraid of the police, so they let him die, then took him and dumped his body by the roadside to make it look like a car accident threw him out of a car.*
>
> *And after, [they] called her [Elda] and told her he had died, OD'd. So, she goes to the funeral with these people.*[21]

But who were "these people?" When I asked Krys for names, she wasn't forthcoming. She only remembered one name which I recognised from when I lived in New York during the early '80s. I don't mention her name here because Krys wasn't sure if Elda had mentioned the person because she was one of the 8 people at the apartment that night or for some other reason. As the woman had something to do with one of Elda's bands, I think it's more likely her name was brought up regarding that.

Krys said that Elda told her that "they" - the people in the room - called her [Elda] when Eric died, but wouldn't that make Elda an accessory to a crime?

---

[21] Krysteen, 10 June 2003 06:54.

Krys said she was outraged "that she [Elda] did nothing about it [the overdose] and she even went with these people" to the funeral. According to Krys, "Elda made it sound like they were the only ones that could get her into the funeral."[22]

Was Krys' comment a confirmation that Elda *was* in the apartment? How could Elda have done anything about the overdose if she wasn't there?

Regarding Elda's lack of help, I wasn't as judgmental as Krysteen. What could anyone have done once Eric injected himself with the fatal dose (if that is what happened)? Eric would have probably been already dead by the time anyone noticed that he was dead; the other people in the room were probably more focused on getting high, themselves, if they weren't already in that state. As noted earlier, heroin overdoses are quick. The drug is injected straight into the bloodstream. It's not like overdosing from pills.

Moving Eric's body didn't necessarily mean his fellow-addicts loved him less; it just meant they didn't want to get into trouble. Overdoses happen. It goes with the territory of being a junkie.

But if Krys was right about Barbara - that she had given Eric too much dope *on purpose* - it would have been pre-meditated murder. Barbara would have

---

[22] Krysteen 10 June 2003 16:40.

wanted the evidence moved out of her apartment as quickly as possible, assuming that it was her and Eric's apartment that he had died in (more on that later).

When Krys referred to Eric's funeral, I wondered whether she was referring to the party/wake that Debbie Harry had referred to previously when she said, "We didn't quite understand what had happened, but we went to a party/wake held for him and saw a lot of people from the earlier glitter days." Elda was part of the "earlier glitter days."

The *Post* article had also mentioned the wake in their article:

> *Eric Emerson was buried on Monday in Wharton, N.J. near his parents' home, following a weekend-long wake. Ronnie Cutrone said that there were plans to videotape the funeral, but they fell through at the last minute...*

The article quotes Cutrone as saying "He [Eric] would have wanted it taped... He would have wanted it like Candy's funeral..."

"Candy" was Candy Darling (born James Slattery) who had appeared as a woman in *Flesh* and *Women in Revolt*, both films produced by Andy Warhol and directed by Paul Morrissey. A biography of Candy

Darling by Cynthia Carr is due to be published in 2024.

Cutrone is described by the *Post* reporters as "a close friend of Emerson's for 10 years and a Warhol associate..."[23] Like Eric, Cutrone was also a junkie; he would go into rehab. in 1980.[24]

During my correspondence with Krysteen, I asked her several times whether she was sure that Eric had overdosed, and she always answered in the affirmative:

> *Yes, again Eric was OD'd and dumped on the side of the road there were 8 people in the house at the time and no one would help him. Barbara did it, Elda says, to keep Eric from seeing Elda and Branch but... I don't know if I believe Elda...*[25]

Was Elda trying to implicate Barbara out of jealousy or was Krysteen trying to implicate Elda out of jealousy? Or both?

In another email, Krys notes Elda's continuing "unhealthy obsession" with Eric:

> *...I see she [Elda] has to this day an*

---

[23] Mel Juffee and Peter Keepnews, "He Brought 'Glitter' to Rock Music, *New York Post*, 4 June 1975, p. 46.
[24] Martin Torgoff, *Can't Find My Way Home: America in the Great Stoned Age, 1945 – 2000* (NY: Simon and Shuster, 2004), p. 374.
[25] Krysteen, 10 June 2003 06:03.

unhealthy obsession with this man [Eric]. She has a fatal attraction kind of liking for him, and I do think in the end it was this that got him killed.

She could never, never, never leave well enough alone. She could not see him with anyone, not just me.

It is really scary talking to her because she lives in her own head about him. Some of the shit she was telling me was so bizarre that I know only a person who is obsessed could talk like that...

Elda told me she had been living with Eric's ghost for 20 years.[26]

The one person who I hadn't been in contact with yet was Elda; I had only heard her side of the story through Krys.

In 2007, after I posted some of the information about Eric's death on my website, Elda emailed me. By then she was working as "Senior Loan Specialist" for a residential home corporation. She might as well have

---

[26] Krysteen, 10 June 2003 03:20.

put down "Dreamer of Dashed Dreams" as her job title. Her new position might have meant a regular pay cheque, but what a comedown after her days as the founder of Pure Garbage. When the lead singer of that band, Holly Woodlawn, died she [Holly} made headlines as the Holly in Lou Reed's song *Walk on the Wild Side*. Debbie Harry from Elda's follow-up band, The Stilettos, went on to fame as the lead vocalist in Blondie. But Elda ended up as a "Senior Loan Specialist," whatever that meant.

Elda wrote:

> *I am the mother of Eric Emerson's son Branch Emerson. My name is Elda Gentile aka Elda Stiletto for the original punk band The Stilettos which launched Debbie Harry's career. I have written a book about the entire inside truth of my life with Eric - a love affair that spanned from 1968 through 1975...*
>
> *P.S. Branch has two beautiful grandchildren. There are also 2 daughters that we found, Erica and Monique who are Branch's stepsisters.*[27]

---

[27] Email from Elda Gentile, 24 January 2007 23:48.

Her book never materialised. When I asked her if she knew Krysteen, she replied:

> *I saw Krysteen for the first time since 1968 about 3 years ago at Grandma Emerson's. Monique had never met Branch or the family before, so we had a big Emerson gathering for a couple of days down in Tennessee. I haven't heard from her since, but I think Branch and Monique are in touch.*[28]

She didn't mention that the gathering took place around the same dates of Eric's death, as Krys had pointed out to me. Unlike what Krys had said - that Eric was just using Elda for a place to stay and for financial support - Elda claimed that she:

> *was Eric's love through all the other women. We both lived with other people at different times but never ended our relationship. Unfortunately, I couldn't stop the down[ward] spiral I saw him spinning into with the funds Barbara Winter provided. I*

---

[28] Elda Gentile, 25 Jan 2007 15:42

> *was devastated by his death, and still have no closure about what really happened to him that night.*[29]

Really? She seemed to know what happened "that night" when she told Krys that Eric had injected himself and that it was Barbara who supplied the dope. "The down[ward] spiral" reference contradicted Debbie Harry's description of Eric "being satisfied... because he had everything..."

Elda said that she still had "no closure about what really happened to him that *night* - a confirmation that it was nighttime when Eric had overdosed even though the *Post* had claimed that his body was found on the roadside in the afternoon. Debbie Harry had also referred to the "night" of his death when Eric had looked "ashen."

* * *

In 2016, Elda's story changed. That year, two years before her death, Elda made a change to Eric's Wikipedia page. She added a quote, by her, about how she had really found out about Eric's death. By that time, I had posted an essay on my site about her previous

---

[29] Email from Elda Gentile, 5 February 2007 18:39.

with the addict turning blue before he/she dies. Although Reed initially uses the pronoun "she" to describe the person who has overdosed, he changes it to "he" at the end of the song, lamenting: "but, oh, how I miss him, baby."

But was Reed describing an incident he was involved in or was he just repeating the rumours that were going around at the time?

On November 14, 2009, I received an email from someone calling themselves "Billy Smith" who copied the quote about Eric's death from *Popism* that I had used on my site and then wrote:

> *The true story was he [Eric] OD'd in Lou Reed's apt. on Spring Street and Lou Reed with the help of a friend put him out on Hudson Street with his bike.*
>
> *Eric and I used to hang out and I remember one night at a summer loft party in Soho we both went out on the fire escape and gave each other a blow job - true story.*[33]

I wrote back and asked, "How do you know that Lou Reed was involved - that he was there at the time?"

---

[33] Email from 'Billy Smith,' 14 November 2009 05:53.

"Billy Smith" replied:

> *A friend of Lou Reed told me when it all happened. It was told to me that Eric and a few guys were there for a day all doing heavy drugs.*
>
> *It was also said to me that Eric was looking for a place to do his drugs and ended up at Reed's place and Eric OD'd in Reed's apt.*
>
> *Reed did not want the publicity and moved the body out to the street with a help of friends during the late night.*"[34]

In his first email, in the "reply to" section, "Billy Smith" had a different email address listed than the one in the "From" section. The "Reply To" email address was "email@billyamato.com." That information did not appear on the second email, after I asked for more details. Billy Amato Smith was the Vice President of 20th Century Fox Records.

He had become the V.P. in 1974, the year before Eric's death. Did his importance in the music business lend credence to his account? Probably. Neither Elda nor

---

[34] Email from 'Billy Smith,' 14 November 2009 17:23.

Krysteen had had mentioned Lou Reed but that didn't mean he wasn't involved.

Unfortunately, Smith's story was hearsay - it had been told to him by somebody else who he didn't identify.

* * *

It is unlikely that the mystery of Eric's death will ever be solved. In a city where dead junkies are a dime a dozen it's doubtful that the NYPD would take the trouble to re-visit Eric's death. Who killed Eric Emerson mostly depends on who you believe, but it's pretty clear that it wasn't a hit and run. Even if he did shoot himself up, the person who provided the dope could still have been done for murder or manslaughter. There was no "Good Samaritan" law in New York then so anyone else in the room could have been arrested too.

Overdoses happen. But whose fault is it? The addict or the person who supplies him with the drugs? How could anyone prove that someone gave Eric too much dope on purpose as Elda claimed in regard to Barbara?

* * *

The more I researched Eric Emerson's death, the more uncomfortable I felt. Even if I had learned who the other people in the room were, would it make a difference? It wouldn't bring Eric back to life. Maybe it didn't matter who was there when he died.

Or maybe I was starting to think like the people in that room. I wondered if by sharing the guilt, they hoped to diminish their individual responsibility for what happened. They didn't see themselves as "guilty." They were just doing what so many of their friends were doing at the time - trying to have fun. Isn't that what everyone wants to have? Fun. Getting high was fun except when things went wrong. But was that anybody's fault?

What had got me interested in the Warhol scene in the first place were all the druggy stories about the Factory - all the wild times. None of Andy Warhol's superstars talked about the bad times when they were interviewed - the times when they couldn't score or when the dope was shit or the overdoses.

The circumstances of Eric's death have become increasingly complicated over time because so many of the players have passed away. Both Krysteen and Elda are dead. Barbara Winter may still be alive but good luck trying to find her. She's been largely written out of Edgar Winter's life and now only appears as a credit on one of his songs. Jane Forth, the mother of Eric's son Emerson Forth, keeps a low profile. Debbie Harry and Blondie, on the other hand, are having a well-deserved claims although there's no way to know whether her Wiki change of story was related to what I had written. She later removed her comments, but they still appear in the page's revision history.

In Wiki, Elda wrote:

> ...*When Barbara Winter contacted me and tried to tell me Eric was hit on his bike I went to Independence Plaza where Eric was staying with her and verified with the door man of the building that he indeed died of an overdose.*
>
> *That evening Barbara [Winter], Ronnie Cutrone and Jane [Forth] came to my apartment not knowing what I knew and upon questioning them I was told there were 8 people hanging out at the apartment when Eric died.*
>
> *I still wonder how the bicycle story came about and live with this tragedy every day.*[30]

---

[30] "Eric Emerson: Difference between revisions," *Wikipedia*, 17 May 2016.
https://en.wikipedia.org/w/index.php?title=Eric_Emerson&oldid=720695333.

Interestingly she names Barbara Winter, Ronnie Cutrone and Jane Forth as the people who told her about the 8 people. She doesn't say explicitly that they were among the people in the apartment, but the inference is there.

The doorman story was new - it wasn't what Elda had told Krys at the reunion. Why change her story?

I also found it strange that Elda's quote on the Wiki page disappeared shortly after it went up. Had someone told her to take it down who realised that it contradicted previous versions of the death? The alibis, if that's what they were, kept on changing.

* * *

My occasional postings about the death of Eric Emerson on my website resulted in more people coming forward with other information.

One popular theory among Lou Reed fans was that Reed's song *Street Hassle* gave the details of Eric's death. Reed's fans had a point. Not only did the song mention an overdose, but also mentions moving the body outside to make it look like a hit and run.

Eric and Lou were friends; both were users, and both had been part of the Warhol crowd. There's a photograph of Lou Reed at Eric's wake on the Getty

Images website.[31]

Even Reed's biographer, Anthony DeCurtis, claims that *Street Hassle* was inspired by Eric's death. For a song inspired by an incident which had been reported in the press as a hit and run, it was very specific about the movement of an overdosed addict's body.

The pronoun of the overdosed person in the song varies between "he" and "she" but this may have been Reed's way of obfuscating who he was talking about or a reference to his and Eric's bisexuality. Both were known to be attracted to men and women. Lou's partner at the time of Eric's death was the 'chick with a dick' Rachel Humphreys. Rachel, whose birth name was Tommy, is presumed to have died of AIDS in 1990. She was buried among other victims of AIDS in Potter's Field.[32]

In *Street Hassle*, Reed begins by singing, "Waltzing Matilda whipped out her wallet/the sexy boy smiled in dismay/She took out four twenties 'cause she liked round figures."

The "sexy boy" makes love to Matilda but suddenly it's noticed that she isn't breathing. The lyrics continue:

---

[31] https://www.gettyimages.co.uk/photos/eric-emerson
[32] Marc Campbell, "Rachel: Lou Reed's Transsexual Muse,"*Dangerous Minds*, 2 June 2013.

> *Hey, that cunt's not breathing/I think she's had too much/of something or other, hey, man, you know what I mean?/*
>
> *I don't mean to scare you/but you're the one who came here/and you're the one who's gotta take her when you leave...*
>
> *you know it could be a hassle/trying to explain this all to a police officer about how it was that your old lady got herself stiffed/And it's not like we could help/but there wasn't nothing no on could do/and if there was, man, you know I would have been the first/*
>
> *But when someone turns that blue/well, its a universal truth/and then you just know that bitch will never fuck again/By the way, that's really some bad shit/that you came to our place with....*

And then this: "... why don't you grab your old lady by the feet/and just lay her out in the darkest street/and by morning, she's just another hit and run."

That's exactly what some people were saying happened to Eric. It's a realistic account of an overdose, resurgence in popularity. During the summer they did a small tour of the UK which included Glastonbury, filmed by the BBC. Chris Stein is still around but his life has been plagued by illness and tragedy. In May of this year (2023) his daughter died of an overdose.[35] His memoir is due in 2024.

With my research finished, I'm left with the niggling feeling that there is still somebody out there who knows exactly what happened all those years ago. At least one of the people who were in the apartment where Eric Emerson overdosed is probably still alive today.

In fact, she might be reading this now.

[end]

---

[35] Anagricel Duran, "Blondie's Debbie Harry speaks out on loss of Chris Stein's daughter, Akira," *NME*, 25th July 2023, https://www.nme.com/news/music/blondies-debbie-harry-speaks-out-on-loss-of-chris-steins-daughter-akira-3473273 (Accessed September 2023)

PART II

Short Stories

The previous narrative *Who Killed Wonderboy?* was factual. The following stories are mostly fiction. The characters and the situations in the following stories do not portray and are not intended to portray any actual persons or parties although they may have been inspired by such.

Morocco

William Burroughs (1954):

I like Tangiers less all the time... The lousy weed tears your throat out like it's cut with horseshit. And no more boot than corn silk. I try to connect for some O, and a citizen sells me some old dried-up poppy pods... One thing I have learned. I know what Arabs do all day and all night. They sit around smoking cut weed and playing some silly card game... They are just a gabby, gossipy simple-minded, lazy crew of citizens... (Incomplete letter from William Burroughs in Tangier to Allen Ginsberg, 26 January 1954)

William Burroughs (1956):

There is something special about Tanger. It is the only place when I am there, I don't want to be any place else. No stasis horrors here. And the beauty of this town that consists in changing combinations... I get an average of ten very attractive propositions a day... (Letter from William

Burroughs in Tangier to Allen Ginsberg, 13 October 1956)

* * *

"Look," Joshua said. "That man is giving you the evil eye."

Gregory looked across the waiting room of the ferry terminal and immediately saw who his friend meant - an old man with an angry forehead and sharp blue eyes that were pointed straight at Greg. He was sitting with a small group of men against the opposite wall dressed in djellabas, their faces lined by the searing heat of the deserts that they grown up in. They looked like workers or traders returning home. They talked animatedly among themselves in a strange dialect, gesticulating with an elegance that seemed almost feminine - except for the man with the evil eye. He wasn't participating in the discussion - he was staring at Greg.

"Don't look," Josh said. Greg changed his focus from the man to the Coke machine next to the man.

"You should be careful when we get to Tangier, regardless of what Burroughs wrote," Josh said.

By "be careful," Joshua meant 'don't act too gay.' Joshua had assumed that the man was giving Greg a dirty look because he was gay. "Burroughs" was the Beat writer William Burroughs. Both travellers were into the Beats. They had never met Burroughs, of course; they had just read *Junkie*, parts of *Naked Lunch* and books about him. Greg had just finished reading a book of letters that Burroughs had written from Tangier in the 1950s. There were a lot of letters to his fellow Beat author, Allen Ginsberg about boys and drugs.

Josh was straight and Greg was gay but that didn't matter. In 1985 there was less of a dividing line between gay and straight than today, at least in New York. Most of the good clubs were gay so straights didn't have much of a choice. A lot of gay guys fancied Josh but he didn't mind. With his floppy brown hair and thick sensual lips, he was used to being looked at. It was his business. He was a model - part of a contingent of English contingent of models who invaded New York in the 1980s.

Gregory wasn't a model. He wasn't anything in particular. He did his best not to work but was sometimes forced by economic circumstances into taking a temp job as a typist. He had taught himself to touch-type in high school on one of those black Underwood typewriters with the mountainous keyboards like the ones in pictures of Jack Kerouac, except that Greg had picked his up at a thrift store.

One night, after an Ecstasy-fuelled conversation about their favourite authors at a club they both frequented in New York called Blunt, they decided to take a two-week holiday in Tangier, to get a taste of what Beats like Burroughs, Kerouac, Ginsberg and Brion Gysin had experienced. It didn't dawn on them that it was more two decades later. A lot can change in two decades, but surprisingly, they would discover that not much had.

A couple of days after their conversation about Burroughs et al., the two friends booked a flight to Algeciras in Spain where they would be able to catch a ferry to Tangier, according to their *Rough Guide to Morocco*.

"Wouldn't you rather go to Marrakesh?" the travel agent asked when they explained their plans.

"No. Tangier. Why Marrakesh?" Josh asked.

"Well, it's just that there's a lot of crime in Tangier."

That's just what they were looking for. Crime. Crime in the form of drugs. Although they had convinced themselves that their main reason for travelling to that city was literary, they were also looking forward to the drugs that Burroughs had written about so freely. Marijuana was still illegal in the States in 1985.

"I'm sure we'll manage," Josh said in his English public-school accent which had melted the travel agent's heart when he had first approached her desk - "I love your accent," she said. Josh smiled politely - how many times had he heard that in New York!

* * *

When the ferry finally arrived at the terminal, Josh and Greg waited behind the other passengers clumsily, the last ones to board. Josh felt embarrassed in his cut-offs - the only passenger wearing shorts - and Gregory wanted to avoid the evil eye man. They found a place to stand on the right-hand side of the deck away from everyone else. By leaning over the rail of the boat, they got the full effect of the breeze created by the ferry as it cut through the small waves made by its motor in the otherwise calm, clear sea. After about half an hour they could see the port of Tangier ahead of them.

"Look," Joshua said. "Dolphins."

A group of dolphins had appeared in the water, leaping next to the boat as if they were guiding it to port. Gregory had never seen real dolphins before; his eyes welled up with tears. He felt like they were welcoming him home - not to New York - but somewhere older than that - an ancient place where the past had begun. He could hear the wailing from the minarets of the Mosques in Tangier, the sound carried by the wind.

Joshua saw Greg's tears and asked what was wrong.

"Nothing is wrong. I don't know. It feels like I'm going back in time. Like this is where I came from."

Josh laughed. "Don't be such a drama queen," he said. "Don't worry, everything will be okay."

He placed his hand on the back of his friend's shoulder, and they watched the dolphins together until the ferry docked. A coach was waiting to take the passengers to the main square in Tangier. It was nearly 100 degrees outside with no air-conditioning in the bus - the Moroccan equivalent was a man in a white djellaba who walked up and down the centre aisle sprinkling the passengers with ice water scented with lemon peels. Joshua and Gregory looked at each other and laughed.

"Genius," Joshua said.

When the bus reached the main square, it was surrounded by young men offering their services as guides. Josh and Greg were an easy mark; their pale faces gave them away as new arrivals. Joshua protested, "No, we don't need a guide. We're not tourists." They wanted to experience the authentic Morocco, like the people who lived there. They didn't need a guide.

"Quick, follow me," Josh said as he pushed his way through the crowd and ran up a nearby street. They walked quickly up the narrow road through the medina, the 'authentic' Tangier, and looked for a room to rent. They came across an old man standing in the doorway of a house with a sign in the window that said 'Pension.' Although the boys didn't speak Arabic, they assumed the sign meant they could rent a room there. As they approached the man to enquire, he waved them off aggressively, shouting "Barbares! Barbares!"

"I think he just called us barbarians," Greg said.

The old man reminded Josh of the guy who gave Greg the evil eye. He had never felt less welcome in a place. He hoped the whole holiday wasn't going to be like this. He didn't want to spend his holiday protecting his friend.

"Maybe we should get a guide after all," Josh said.

They walked back to where the coach had dropped them off and found a guide who spoke English.

"We need a hotel," Josh said, preparing to be ripped off. "But not a tourist hotel. We want to stay in a Moroccan hotel. We're not tourists."

The guide, who was about the same age as Joshua - Greg was about five years older - smiled broadly, happy to help.

"Hotel?" he repeated.

"Yes, but not a tourist place," Josh repeated.

"No. No tourist hotel," the guide reassured him. "You can trust. Follow."

They followed him to a hotel near the square - a western-style hotel that catered to tourists - exactly what they were trying to avoid.

"But this is a tourist hotel." Joshua complained. "We want a Moroccan one."

"Yes, yes. Moroccan hotel. Real Moroccan hotel." the guide said, smiling sincerely.

It didn't look like a Moroccan hotel; it looked like the

type of place you'd see in American movies from the 1950s that catered to traveling salesmen. The lobby wallpaper wasn't exactly peeling, but it looked like it was about to. There was also a bar in the lobby selling alcohol, which Joshua thought was unusual for a "real Moroccan hotel." He thought Muslims weren't allowed to drink - that's why they smoked spliff.

The guide introduced them to the manager who happened to be his friend. The room was so cheap that they took it even though it was clearly not a traditional hotel. Joshua wondered how many times the guide had been asked by tourists for a 'real' Moroccan hotel before being taken to this one - which happened to be managed by the guide's friend.

As they signed the register and handed over their passports the manager signalled for the porter - a long-haired teenager - to take their luggage to the room. Fearing an eventual request for a tip, Joshua insisted that they could carry their own luggage. Being English, he didn't believe in tipping. He hated how Americans tipped so freely. He never tipped in England and whenever he had to do it in New York, he felt like he had been punched in the stomach. Besides, what was referred to as their "luggage" was only Joshua's duffel bag and Gregory's backpack. As they reached down to pick them up, they realised that the porter was already holding the bags hostage in front of the elevator.

They paid for one night at the hotel, figuring they could always book more nights if needed, and thanked the guide. He smiled, shook their hands enthusiastically, and stood patiently waiting for a tip. Gregory handed him a considerable number of coins from his pocket, not knowing how much they were worth, but when the guide approached Joshua, he scowled and shook his head 'no.' The guide bowed slightly and waved as he went out the door. "See you later," he said, staring at Joshua. It sounded like a threat.

The elevator arrived and the porter called to them, "Come. Come."

"I'm coming, I'm coming," Gregory joked suggestively. (Nobody laughed.)

Once in the elevator, Greg tried to engage the porter in conversation, using the French he had learned at university. The porter scrunched up his face trying to understand. Apparently Moroccan French was different than university French, at least the way that Gregory spoke it.

The porter carried their bags to their room and stood waiting for the inevitable tip. Joshua ignored him and Gregory was forced to do the tipping again. As the porter was leaving, Greg had an idea. "Excuse me," he said.

The porter turned around: "Yes?"

"Uh, we were wondering... you wouldn't happen to

know where we could get some marijuana, would you?"

Joshua froze. He pretended he wasn't listening; he busied himself by studying his reflection in a large mirror hanging above a dilapidated wooden dresser.

Gregory had assumed that because the porter was young and had long hair, he would know where to score. It was a risk, of course - he could have reported them to the manager, but Greg figured that if they were going to score, it would be safer to score from someone who worked at the hotel they were staying in. There was less of a chance of being ripped off. If the porter complained, they could always say that there had been a misunderstanding because of the language and take their business elsewhere.

"Mira wanna?" the porter asked in broken English. Then he realised what Gregory was talking about. "Oh, hashish?"

"Yes, hashish!" Greg said.

"Yes. I have a friend," the porter said. "He has hashish. He will meet you in front of the hotel in trente minutes. OK?"

"What is his name?" Greg asked.

"Name? Mohammed."

"What does he look like?"

"Look? Yes, look in thirty minutes," he replied, holding up three fingers on his right hand and then a zero formed by the fingers of his left hand. "Outside hotel. He will know you."

"Thank you. That's very nice of you," Greg said and gave him another tip.

After the porter left, Joshua shouted "Yes!" and rubbed his hands together excitedly. The holiday was about to begin.

* * *

Greg and Joshua didn't need to find Mohammed. He found them. The two pale Westerners weren't difficult to notice. Mohammed was older than Greg expected - probably in his forties - and he was wearing a dark grey suit instead of a djellaba. The suit had seen better days. With its large lapels, it looked about a decade out of style.

"Hotel friend?" he asked.

"Yes," Gregory answered. "Are you Mohammed, the porter's friend?"

"Yes. Me ist Mohammed. Follow."

They followed.

They went down the main road, turned left at the first intersection, then right and left again (or was it another right?). Round and round they went inside the medina, down nameless roads that led to nowhere in particular. Mohammed stopped in front of a rug shop and motioned for them to go in.

"But" Joshua protested. "We want hashish, not rugs."

Mohammed looked around cautiously and said, "yes hashish. Here." He motioned again for them to go in. They walked toward the back of the shop where, behind some hanging rugs, a group of old men were sitting on cushions arranged in a circle on the floor. They were passing a hash pipe to each other and welcomed the newcomers with mostly toothless smiles.

"You try first," Mohammed said. "Sit."

Greg turned to Joshua, "How civilised, he wants us to try before we buy."

Joshua looked uncomfortable as they squeezed themselves into the circle. The men laughed as they made room for them. They passed the pipe to their guests as Mohammed went into a room in the back of the shop and returned with a tray of mint tea. Gregory felt completely at ease sitting on the large cushions, surrounded by Moroccan carpets, but Joshua was worried. Neither of them knew where they were or how they would get back to the hotel without Mohammed's help.

Gregory got stoned quickly. As he sipped his tea, he couldn't help but comment loudly, "This is great! Who would have thought that a cup of hot tea would be just the thing needed to cool down on such a hot day!" The old men laughed, not understanding a word.

Josh was afraid that they were laughing at his friend

rather than with him. He was determined to keep his wits about him in case there was trouble. But the more he smoked the funnier everything became. The Moroccans didn't understand the two visitors and Greg and Josh didn't understand the Moroccans, but anything anyone said or did resulted in gales of laughter from everyone. At the height of the hilarity, Mohammed left again and came back with the owner of the shop who was carrying a considerable assortment of rugs.

"He wants you to buy," Mohammed said to Greg and Joshua.

There was no way that they were going to buy the rugs. They were cheap imitations of the authentic kilims that surrounded them. They looked more like the polyester rugs you could buy on 14th Street for $14.99, but with price tags about ten times that amount.

When they told the shop owner they weren't interested, he tried to haggle with them. "You don't understand," Joshua said. "We don't want any rugs."

The owner left and came back with another selection of overpriced rugs. The old men laughed. When those rugs were rejected, more rugs were produced.

Joshua tried another tactic: "We can't afford rugs. We're not rich tourists. We're poor students."

The shop owner didn't fall for it. Westerners were, by definition, rich. They existed to be ripped off. He brought out more rugs. The old men laughed again.

Joshua had had enough. He stood up and shouted louder than he meant to: "WE DON'T WANT RUGS! WE WANT HASHISH!"

The old men stopped laughing. They didn't like the shouting. "Maybe you shouldn't have mentioned hashish," Gregory whispered.

Mohammed motioned for Joshua and Greg to follow him through a door in the back wall which led to a small, empty room. Mohammed closed the door and reached into the crotch of his trousers and brought out a large brick of hash.

"My god, it's so big!" Gregory exclaimed.

"He had it with him the entire time." Joshua whispered. He calmly explained to Mohammed that they were only in Morocco for two weeks and that they didn't need that much hash. They only needed a quarter of an ounce or so for their holiday, not a whole kilo.

Mohammed suggested that they take whatever they didn't smoke back to New York with them: "You can sell in New York," he said. "Easy." He began to explain how they could get it through customs "easy," but they told him they weren't interested; they only wanted a small amount. He didn't look pleased. "Follow," he said.

They followed. They assumed that Mohammed was going to get a knife to cut off a small amount from the large brick he had put back into his trousers. They walked behind him as he left the shop through a back door and down another series of narrow streets, and then another. The further they went into the medina, the scarier it got and the fewer limbs people seemed to have - beggars with one arm and a dark socket for an eye.

Gregory looked at a one-eyed beggar and asked Joshua, "Do you think that was a result of an 'eye for an eye?' Isn't that what they believe in? It doesn't feel very safe around here, wherever we are."

Joshua told him to shut up, and not to look at anyone. "Some of the men are carrying daggers," he warned.

Gregory looked around at the men whose hungry eyes were following them. Tangier suddenly seemed a long way from Manhattan.

As the beggars and thieves came closer, Mohammed seemed to lose the ability to speak English. When Josh asked where they were or where the hotel was, he remained silent and led them further and further into the abyss of the medina.

'What do we do now?' the boys eyes asked each other. Josh kept his cool. Gregory went for the chaos option. He fell to his knees in the middle of the road and cried out loudly, "Help! I'm sick! I need my medicine from the hotel!"

Joshua knew that his friend was faking it but didn't know what his part was supposed to be in the drama. When he bent down to help him get up, Greg stayed right where he was and screamed even louder: "Help! Help! I'm dying!"

The beggars and thieves were confused; they chatted amongst themselves in Darija. Nobody wanted a dead American on their hands; nor did they want the unnecessary attention a dead American would bring to their street and its illegalities.

Mohammed began to worry. The same eyes that had looked threateningly at the Americans earlier were now looking disparagingly at him. Why was he not giving the American his medicine? Why had he brought trouble to their street? Mohammed was worried that Greg might have AIDS. His friend, the hotel porter, had told him the travellers were from New York.

"Come, come," he said to Greg. "We go to hotel."

Greg looked upward at his saviour. "The hotel where we are staying?" he asked.

"Yes, yes. The hotel where you stay," Mohammed answered.

Josh helped Gregory up and they followed Mohammed back to the hotel. The beggars and thieves watched with relief as the the troublemakers turned the corner, freeing the locals to return to whatever dubious activities they had been up to before all the drama began. Now it became a story that they told their friends about later.

Greg and Joshua weren't as far from the hotel as they

thought. The reason that it felt like they had been going in circles before was because they were. Civilisation was only a few streets away. They even passed a group of tourists on a walking tour. When they were across the street from their hotel, Mohammed handed them the block of hash from his trousers and asked for $35.00. They looked at each other, both thinking the same thing - if they had known it was so cheap, they would have just bought the whole block in the first place. $35.00 was how much a quarter would cost in New York.

Once they were safely ensconced in their room, Joshua and Gregory couldn't believe their luck. Josh threw the block of hash on his bed and started to roll out a joint. There were two beds, but he motioned for Greg to join him on his - it would be easier to pass the joint that way. Gregory took his *Rough Guide* out of his knapsack and laid down next to his friend. Finally, it felt like the holiday was really beginning.

When they finished smoking the first joint, they rolled a second, stronger one. While reading his guide, Gregory came across a sentence that they had first read in New York that warned tourists not to buy drugs in Morocco. He showed it to Josh - "Remember this?" he asked laughing.

Then they read the next paragraph which they had previously passed over - about how the dealers sold the stuff and then accepted bribes from the police to reveal who they sold it to. The cops didn't get into trouble and the dealers got paid twice; it was the customers who got busted.

"Maybe that was why Mohammed insisted we buy a whole brick," Josh said. "The larger amount of dope, the bigger the bribe."

They read and re-reread the paragraph and each time it got worse. It seemed to describe their exact circumstance. It even said not to trust the hotel you are staying in. The staff could be working with the police. They looked at the large brick of hash on the bed which had looked so inviting a few minutes ago. Now it looked more like evidence. They had to get rid of it quickly, before the police arrived.

"Just throw it out the window, Joshua. It's too risky to hold onto it," Gregory said.

"Are you mad!" Joshua asked, meaning 'crazy.' There was no way that he was going to waste $35.00. He looked out the window on the other side of the room and saw a series of intersecting pipes. Wrapping the brick up in a hotel towel. he stuck it behind the pipes. If the police arrived, at least the hash wouldn't be in their room. They wouldn't be able to prove it was theirs - unless of course the police noticed a towel was missing from their room.

"Let's get something to eat," Joshua suggested. "I'm starving."

"Me too."

They decided, with everything they'd been through that day to treat themselves to a large Moroccan meal at a traditional restaurant. They didn't care about the price - they just wanted authenticity. It would be their first meal in the country. They took the stairs to the lobby thinking it would be safer, less noisy, than the elevator. They were very stoned and very paranoid and the last thing they wanted was attention. Once in the lobby they slid past the bar to the exit.

"Don't look now, but there's Mohammed," Joshua said, nodding toward the bar.

Gregory saw Mohammed talking to a group of men in suits in the lobby bar which included the hotel manager. Scoring through the hotel porter didn't seem so safe now. If Mohammed was a friend of the manager, how safe could it be? Maybe they were all part of the same gang.

Mohammed walked over to the two travellers and greeted them as if they were old friends, shaking their hands like a westerner. Then he got down to business. He wanted more money.

"But we paid you already!" Joshua protested.

"I need more," Mohammed demanded.

Joshua held his ground. He repeated that they had already paid him. Mohammed replied with something that sounded like a parable - "If you pay more, you sleep in peace with both eyes closed but, if you not pay, you sleep with only one eye." Then he opened his jacket to reveal the handle of a large knife sticking out of the inside pocket.

Joshua stuck his chest out and demanded to know if Mohammed was threatening them.

Mohammed answered, "Yes, yes, I threaten you."

"Oh."

Gregory couldn't cope. "I can't cope! Just give him more money!" he shouted to Josh as he rushed back to the elevator to return to the safety of their room. When he reached it, he jumped into bed and pulled the bedspread over himself, trying not to think about anything. If he didn't think about it, maybe it wouldn't happen - whatever 'it' was.

The room door eventually opened, and somebody came in. Greg tried to make himself as flat as possible.

"You can come out now," Josh said. "It's only me."

"What happened?" Greg asked, as came out from under the bedspread.

"I had to haggle. But we still had to pay an extra twenty. You owe me a tenner."

Greg sat on the side of the bed, relieved that nothing worse had happened.

"Don't worry. I'll cash some traveller's checks at the restaurant. Are you we still going out to eat?"

"Yeah, of course. Let's just wait a bit. To give him

time to leave."

They checked the dope to make sure it was still in its hiding place and smoked another joint - "we might as well," Josh said, then went back downstairs. No Mohammed. They walked around outside for a while but couldn't find a restaurant that looked particularly Moroccan. They ended up at a burger joint. Maybe there weren't any traditional restaurants anymore, or maybe the burger joint was a traditional restaurant. It was filled with Moroccans.

The following morning, they woke up early, smoked a joint, and quickly checked out of the hotel. The manager leaned over the counter as he handed over their passports.

"Did you enjoy your stay in Tangier?" his looming face asked with an ominous smile.

They didn't answer; they just grabbed their passports and ran to the coach stop as quickly as they could. For all they knew, the manager could be ringing his friend Mohammed to let him know that they were headed to the main square so that he could extort more money out of them.

The square was as chaotic as ever, with people rushing from one bus to another, trying to find out which one went to their destination. There were no printed timetables. Greg and Joshua saw a coach that was about to leave with a handwritten sign in the window that said "Asilah" in several languages.

"I think that's where *Suddenly Last Summer* was filmed," Gregory said. "It was supposed to be Spain, but it was really filmed there."

"What's *Suddenly Last Summer*?" Joshua asked.

"An old Hollywood movie with Anthony Perkins and Elizabeth Taylor. It's on TV sometimes. Anthony Perkins gets chased and eaten by a bunch of boys wanting money or something like that."

"Great."

"The town is supposed to be beautiful. It's on the coast."

The bus was about to leave. They got on. They didn't want risk another minute in Tangier.

* * *

Most of the visitors to Asilah in the 1980s were Moroccans or families visiting from other Arabic countries. There weren't many European visitors at all; Americans were even rarer. The main plaza, where the busses stopped, was similar to the one in Tangier. Once again, as they left their bus, they were deluged by young men wanting to be their guides. But the Asilah guides were better looking than the ones in Tangier. Greg doubted that these boys would cannibalise anyone. They were more like laid-back surfers than cannibals.

Maybe it was the result of the sea air. You couldn't see the ocean from the main square, but you could certainly feel it. It felt like freedom; like the dolphins leaping freely in the sea next to the ferry boat when they first arrived.

The square was surrounded by cafes like the square in Tangier had been - full of men drinking tea and playing cards or a board game that looked like checkers. Nobody rushed to do anything; time passed without anyone noticing. Gregory and Josh sat down at a cafe and ordered mint tea. Young men approached their table with offers of places to stay and Greg asked a good-looking Moroccan in his early twenties to join them. They ordered another tea and Gregory tried to make small talk with the Moroccan. "It's so much nicer here than Tangier..." he said, but all he got was a blank stare. He thought he might have better luck with a direct question, so he asked the guide for his name.

"Mohammed," the guide answered.

"Not another one...." Joshua muttered under his breath.

"Why is everyone called Mohammed?" Greg asked. The guide laughed but didn't answer.

Joshua looked at the men drinking tea in the cafes around them. "Doesn't anybody work?" he asked the guide.

Mohammed shrugged.

They explained that they were looking for a room near the beach in an authentic Moroccan house, that they didn't have much money and that they weren't tourists. "No problem," the guide responded. After they finished their tea, he asked them to "follow." They followed.

Joshua said, "Here we go again."

After a short walk to the beach, their guide stopped and pointed. "There" he said.

Josh and Greg couldn't believe their luck. They would be renting a room in a house that was literally, on the beach - with a front door that opened onto the sand and beyond that was the sea.

Joshua began to haggle over the price which seemed a bit steep by Moroccan standards, but as they haggled it became clear that Mohammed was renting them the whole house, not just a room; rather than being expensive, it was a bargain.

"Even if we visit other parts of the country, we can use the house as a base," Josh said to Greg.

As they got closer to the house, however, they could see there were already people living in it. A woman was talking to a group of children, presumably her own. Joshua turned to Mohammed: "But there are people living there."

"No problem," Mohammed answered, and went inside to talk to the woman with the kids. It wasn't long before she came out with the kids, all of them carrying cushions and small pieces of furniture which they set up in the front of the house.

Joshua turned to Gregory: "He's moving the family out so that we can move in."

Greg replied, "That's absurd. We can't do that!"

They called Mohammed over and explained that they couldn't force the family to move just so they could have a place to stay during their holiday. He told them not to worry; that families often rented out their homes during the summer to make extra money. The woman was smiling at them as she brought out more cushions and blankets. She certainly didn't seem offended.

For the next two weeks the family lived in the front of the house under the living room window, cooking on a small bonfire and sleeping on the cushions. The kids looked like they were having a great time camping out, running freely and playing chasing games but after a few days they wanted to watch television - there was an old black and white TV indoors - so Gregory let them in to watch TV. Then their mother wanted to use the kitchen, so Gregory let her use the kitchen. In the end, it was difficult to tell whether Gregory and Josh were guests of the family, or the other way round. Greg loved being part of a local family but wasn't so sure how Joshua felt about it. He heard his friend using the word "mental" a lot as the screaming kids chased each other down the hallway.

Gregory tended to wake up with the sun; Joshua stayed in bed until the sun became unbearable. Every morning, Greg would take his place on the wide ledge of the open window of the living room and smoke a joint and drink mint tea that the family prepared over their fire. The beach was so quiet at that time; small waves lapped the shore lightly without a sunbather in sight. Looking out on the empty sea was like staring into eternity. He couldn't remember when he had last felt so happy.

By the time that Joshua got out of bed, people were already arriving on the beach. Greg and he sunbathed every day in the same location - on a small corner of sand away from the water. It wasn't as popular as the area closer to the sea, but Josh wanted to avoid attention, especially with Gregory in his white speedos. That swimsuit might be okay for Fire Island, but this was a Muslim beach full of women sunbathing in burqas and men in djellabas guiding camels through the sand.

"It's like sunbathing in the Middle Ages," Joshua said when he saw the camels. "Mental."

* * *

Josh could sunbathe for hours, lying motionless on the beach under a pair of Ray Bans, as he worked on his tan for the inevitable return to New York. Gregory got bored easily. He liked to sit up and watch the people on the rest of the beach. He wondered why Joshua always insisted that they sunbathe so far away from everyone else.

On their last day of sunbathing, a fight broke out between two men on the beach. It was like something out of *The Arabian Nights*. The men were dressed in baggy harem trousers and heavily decorated tunics despite the hot sunshine. The fight began with them shouting at each other; then one of them pulled out a long, curved sword from his belt and waved it in the air. The other man immediately did the same, both still shouting at each other. The argument almost became a dance.

"Joshua, wake up!" Gregory screeched. "There's a fight going on with machetes!"

Joshua sat up. "Good Lord," he said, watching the men swinging their swords at each other. "Don't look!"

Gregory couldn't help watching the drama develop; other sunbathers hardly paid attention - as if they saw this type of thing every day. A woman in a burqa ran to one of the men and got down on her knees in front of him. Raising her arms to the sky, presumably in the direction of Allah, she appeared to be begging for the fighting to stop. Another woman did the same in front of the other man. There was a lot of wailing, but nobody seemed to know what to do next. It was like they were following a script and had run out of lines. "Let's get out of here," Joshua said. They gathered their belongings and headed into town.

As they walked along the pathway at the back of the beach, a group of young Moroccan men started following them. Joshua was surprised by their swimsuits which were even skimpier than Greg's. The material was so thin and cheap that you could see through it. Gregory couldn't take his eyes off their slim, smooth bodies. The Moroccans appeared to enjoy the attention, smiling flirtatiously. Joshua ignored them and warned Gregory to "hurry up."

Greg hurried up, even though his attention was elsewhere: "My god, they could be models if they were in New York," he said to Joshua. "They're beautiful."

There was one bather who was particularly striking. A tall guy in red Speedos, probably in his early twenties, with thick black hair pushed back from his forehead, who looked back at Gregory with a "dazzling" smile. Greg remembered Burroughs describing the smile of a young man in Morocco that way - "dazzling" - in a letter to Allen Ginsberg. There was another line from a Burroughs letter that Greg tried to recall - something about how "innocence was inseparable from depravity..."

"Stop flirting," Josh said. "You're going to get us both

into trouble."

"But they're beautiful."

Josh cringed. "They might be beautiful now, but eventually they'll be just like those dried-out old men in the ferry terminal."

'How sad that those beautiful boys would end up so old and grey,' Gregory thought. But then, what about himself and Josh? As their futures became their past, what would happen to them? Wouldn't they just become a new version of their parents?

Because he was gay, Gregory felt protected from the repetitive cycle of heterosexuality. Gay marriage didn't exist in 1985. Greg's gay friends in New York wanted to be accepted as they were; they didn't want to emulate the straight world. Greg made a vow to himself to remember the swimmer's smile forever. Joshua yelled at him to hurry up "before we both get stabbed!"

Gregory stuck his tongue out at him. One of the Moroccans saw and rushed to tell his friends what had happened. They laughed and waved a final good-bye before diving into the sea. Greg waved back and caught up with Joshua who warned him to be careful - that homosexuality was still illegal in Morocco. He had read it in the guidebook.

They continued walking until they arrived at their usual cafe in town. There wasn't anything special about it; they had gone there once at the beginning of their holiday and there didn't seem to be a reason to go anywhere else. The owner always greeted them with a smile and brought them glasses of mint tea without having to be asked. They sat silently, drinking their tea, watching the hubbub of the village in front of them.

Gregory liked how the Moroccan men walked around with their arms over each other's shoulders. It reminded him of when he was a kid and he and his best friend, Billy Pereira, would walk around their neighbourhood that way. He hadn't seen Billy since they were teenagers. Greg and his family had moved before then, but they still visited the old neighbourhood occasionally.

The last time they visited, Billy took Gregory into his bedroom and brought out a shoe box hidden behind some clothes on the top shelf of a closet. Inside the box was a syringe and a small envelope of brown powder. He shot up in front of Greg like he was showing off. He must have been about sixteen at the time. Greg felt sorry for his friend; only 'bad' people did hard drugs. But now, in New York, people used heroin to come down from cocaine and ecstasy, and it didn't seem like such a big deal. He wondered what had become of his childhood friend; for all he knew, Billy, who was a Mexican, was still living in the run-down area of Pacoima that Gregory's family, who were white, later characterised as a slum.

The shadow of a hand passed over Greg's face. It was Joshua. "Wakey - wakey!" he said, waking Greg up from his daydream. Since arriving in Morocco Greg's thoughts often drifted; his sense of time became confused, as if the past, present and future were blending into each other. Everything seemed so temporary. Today would be tomorrow in no time at all, the distant past felt like yesterday but the 'real' yesterday seemed like such a long time ago.

Gregory returned to the 'here and now' and apologised for being so spaced out - "it must be the sun." They ordered more tea and watched the street performers in front of them - mostly kids doing magic tricks or dancing for tips. One young boy had wrapped a cloth around himself like a sari and was belly dancing, much to the delight of the Moroccan men sitting on the street curb, encouraging him with their claps; not many of the men had money to give him, but he enjoyed the attention. After one dance he walked straight up to Joshua and opened his small hand as wide as he could, hoping for a tip. Joshua shook his head 'no' as Gregory reached into his bag and gave him all the coins his little hand could hold. The boy was overjoyed. He gave Greg a "dazzling" smile and blinked his eyes coquettishly before starting a new dance.

"What the fuck?" Joshua asked, surprised by the boy's response.

Gregory laughed. He believed that 'campness' should be encouraged at any age. The boy continued dancing. Joshua told Greg to hurry up and finish his tea so they could get back to the house. As they were leaving, Gregory found more coins in his bag and handed them to the boy in mid-dance. The audience applauded wildly as if Gregory had become a part of the show. He bowed slightly to thank them. Josh wanted to disappear.

"Don't encourage them!" Joshua whispered loudly.

"Don't be so cheap," Gregory said.

As the two travellers got nearer to home, they noticed a small group of young Moroccans waiting for them. Greg and Josh had got into the habit of going to a small café on the beach at night where the owner didn't mind if they smoked hash. The smell had attracted the young Moroccans and they ended up joining Josh and Greg at their table. After that first night they met every night at the cafe, smoking, drinking mint tea and playing cards to the calming sounds of eternity lapping at the shore.

Joshua didn't mind sharing their spliff because they had so much, and he liked entertaining the Moroccans with stories about the fashion industry. But Josh and Greg had never met them in the daylight and were surprised to see them waiting outside the house they were renting. Nobody else was around. The family must have gone to the market. One rule that they had agreed to when renting out the property was that they weren't allowed to have Moroccans in the house.

"I'm sorry," Joshua said to the young men, "But we're not allowed to have visitors in the house."

"Yes, of course," one of the Moroccans said. "That is usually the rule. Would you like to walk with us on the beach?"

Before Greg could say yes, Josh said no, that they would see them later at the cafe, as usual.

"We're going home tomorrow," Greg added.

"Yes, we know."

The boys looked at each other, shuffling their feet in the sand, trying to decide who would talk first. Finally, one of them got up the courage to ask if they could have some hashish - "just enough for one joint," he asked politely, in English.

"Sure," Josh said. He took a joint from his bag and handed it to them.

"Thank you. We will see you at the cafe later, if that is okay."

"Yes, of course," the travellers answered. The Moroccans smiled and went their way. One winked at Greg as he was leaving.

"I saw that," Josh said as they went into the house.

They had only been inside for a few minutes when there was a light tapping at the door. It was the boy who had winked at Greg. Josh looked for the others and saw them further down the beach, smoking the joint he had given them.

"I told them I was asking for more hashish," the Moroccan at the door said. "But I need to tell you something. You are nice people."

"Yes?" Josh said, with Gregory peering over his shoulder.

"The others. Because you are leaving tomorrow, they say that they are going to steal your hashish and money tonight. And are going to rape you."

"They wot!?" Joshua asked.

"That's their plan," the Moroccan said.

Joshua thanked the Moroccan for letting them know and started to close the door.

"Would it be possible to get some more hashish?" the Moroccan quickly asked, "So they won't think I came to warn you?"

He held out his hand. Greg went to the kitchen where they kept the rest of the block and cut off a sizeable amount for him.

"Thank you." The boy ran off to his friends, and then yelled back, "see you later at the cafe. OK?"

Gregory smiled and said yes, that they would see them later.

Joshua shut the door and sat down in the front room to roll as joint.

"What do you think?" he asked with a worried

frown.

"You know, despite everything," Gregory answered. "I'd still trust those Moroccans more than most New Yorkers I know. I've never felt so safe."

Joshua called him "hopeless," and finished rolling the joint.

* * *

Josh and Greg didn't allow the prospect of rape and robbery to ruin the last evening of their holiday. Gregory still invited their Moroccan friends to their table to play cards, drink tea and smoke, and Joshua continued to entertain them with stories about the fashion world. They left Asilah the next morning. The Moroccan boys met them to say good-bye and went with them to the coach stop. Josh gave them what was left of the brick. Waving at them through the window of the coach as it drove off, Greg felt like he was going to cry. Although he had only known them for a couple of weeks, they felt like lifelong friends. They waved back from the pavement, and he imagined they felt the same. Joshua was reading a book and didn't bother to wave. When he looked up, he saw the sadness on Gregory's face and asked him what was wrong "this time." When Greg tried to explain, Joshua laughed: "What a load of bullocks. They'll just go on to the next batch of tourists when we're gone. They won't even remember us in a week."

Joshua went back to his book. He had brought quite a few paperbacks to read on holiday but hadn't started reading them until now. Greg looked at the front cover - the *Heart of Darkness* by Joseph Conrad. He asked if it was good, and Joshua was shocked that he hadn't read it before. "This is my second time," he explained. "I read it in school the first time. It's excellent. You should read it. Everyone should."

Their trip back to New York was fairly uneventful. They returned to Tangier where they got the coach to the ferry terminal. Nobody bothered them this time. Maybe they could tell by their tans that they weren't new arrivals. The ferry going back to Spain wasn't accompanied by dolphins as the one going to Morocco had been, and the ferry terminal was fairly empty. No evil eyes. They arrived at the airport early and had a long sleep on the plane. The next night they went to Blunt.

Gregory felt like they had been away for such a long time. When people asked about the trip, he said it was the best holiday he had ever been on but couldn't explain why. He wasn't sure how Joshua felt. He heard him complaining to some friends that the holiday had been "a bore." Greg thought Josh might have been disappointed because they hadn't seen more of the sights, but as far as Greg was concerned, he could have spent the rest of his life drinking mint tea and playing cards with their young Moroccan friends on the beach. Years later, when he wrote this story, he still wished that he had never left.

[end]

Selma Avenue

When Paul Holloway was growing up in a suburb of a suburb of Los Angeles, the only thing he could think of was escape. As a teenager during the early 1970s, he spent most of his time in his bedroom, reading books about the wider - and wilder - world outside; stories that usually involved sex or drugs or rock and roll, which was the world he really wanted to experience. Unfortunately for him, his parents loved living in the suburbs; they thought they had achieved the American dream. They loved the orange groves, the parks and the tree-lined streets. Paul hated nature - absolutely despised it. The only thing that orange groves were good for, in his opinion, were for smoking joints with his friends. He craved a concrete jungle. He found it, at least temporarily, in the pages of John Rechy's account of the hustler world - *City of Night*. He thought that hustling might provide him with an escape from his suburban prison, but when he left home and moved to Hollywood, about an hour's drive from where grew up, he lacked the courage of his convictions. Instead of becoming a hustler, he became a bank teller.

In Hollywood, he lived in a studio apartment at the foot of the Hollywood Hills, not far from Selma Avenue which Rechy had mentioned in his book as a street where male prostitutes plied their trade. Every morning, Paul drove down Selma on his way to the bank, feeling like a cowardly voyeur as he watched the "youngmen" (as Rechy called them) on the street, not knowing whether they were beginning their day or ending it. Probably there were unlucky ones who had been there all night, but he imagined that most of them had been dropped off after a wild all-night pool party at the home of whatever Hollywood producer had picked them up the night before. He wished he had the courage to join them. He was tired of following the same routine - waking up at 7 so he could get to the bank by 8. The prostitutes on Selma didn't have to follow an alarm clock.

Selma wasn't the only street where you could find male prostitutes in Hollywood, of course, but the prostitutes on Selma were different than the ones that hung out closer to the mainstream gay scene on Santa Monica Boulevard. The Selma prostitutes looked like straight guys who had just arrived on a Greyhound from the mid-west; probably a lot of them had. Paul envied their comraderie. When they weren't trying to attract "scores," as Rechy's hustlers called their customers, they huddled in small groups like brothers, probably comparing notes. Paul wanted to be part of that brotherhood.

If he was going to take the plunge into their exciting world, it would have to be soon. He wasn't getting any younger. He looked young but he was already in his late twenties, nearing that in-between age of thirty when he'd be too old to hustle but too young to be a "score."

* * *

One Saturday morning, after yet another dull night out on the mainstream gay scene, Paul made the decision: "Okay," he told himself, "This is it. Today is the day I am going to stop thinking about becoming a prostitute and actually do it."

He started getting ready at 4:00 pm. He wanted to get to Selma Avenue by 5:00 when it would still be light out. It probably wasn't the way most prostitutes thought, but he couldn't help but worry about being mugged in the dark. Also, there was bound to be a pre-dinner crowd of potential customers around that time; maybe he'd be treated to a meal in a star-studded restaurant in addition to any other money he made.

After a shower, Paul stood in front of his bedroom mirror trying to decide what to wear. Underwear was a problem - to wear or not to wear? And if to wear, what would show off his bulge the best? After rejecting a skimpy pair of bikini-type underwear (too femme) and a jockstrap (too backless), he finally decided on a normal pair of stretchy boxer shorts. It didn't show off his bulge, but he hoped that by clinching the waist of whatever jeans he decided to wear, he could accentuate his manhood underneath.

He tried on various jeans, but they all looked so clean. They lacked the "slept-in" look that seemed so popular on Selma. He had bought a UCLA sweatshirt at a thrift store, thinking that potential customers might be turned on by a student, but he was so skinny that when he put it on, his chest disappeared; on the gay scene he was considered a "twink." There was a demand for twinks, but twinks never thought about it that way. They felt too skinny to be attractive.

He finally decided to wear what he was wearing before his shower - a navy blue t-shirt and a pair of stone-washed Levis. He couldn't remember if his cock should go on the left or right side - which side was passive and which was active? It fell naturally to the right side, and it looked bigger on that side, so he left it there.

As he strolled down to Selma, he occasionally rubbed his bulge with his arm to make it look bigger, but he needn't have worried; the street was empty. There was no "pre-dinner" crowd. He walked down one side of the street and then up the other side, hoping something would happen. A car appeared and slowed down, but then quickly sped up as it passed. He felt rejected. After about an hour, he gave up. He was bored. Of all the worries and expectations that he had about becoming a prostitute, boredom hadn't been one of them. He decided to go home; at least he had tried.

As soon as he turned the corner at Vine Street on his way home, an expensive-looking sports car slowed down and stopped just ahead of him. His luck had, apparently, changed. A car like that could only belong to a millionaire, probably somebody in the movie business, he thought. He walked quickly - almost ran - to it and jumped into the passenger side. The door had been left partially open. He barely had time to close it before they drove off.

Inside the car, Paul turned to look at the "score." The first thing he noticed was the toupée that slanted slightly to the right. Then there was the score's age and weight; he was at least thirty years older than Paul and so overweight that Paul wondered how he had got into such a small car in the first place. The steering wheel disappeared into the driver's stomach as mounds of white, pasty flesh cascaded over the car's stick shift like out-of-control yogurt.

Placing his plump hand on Paul's leg so gently that it only increased the nausea that Paul already felt, he asked, "What's up?" like a teenager might ask another teenager but coming off as more creepy than cool.

There was no way Paul could go through with this; he told the driver that he was on his way home. "I only live up there," he said, pointing to nowhere in particular. "You can drop me off here," he added nervously.

The driver looked puzzled. "That's okay. I can take you home," he said. "Or do you want to go to my place? You'd like it there. I have a pool. Do you like champagne?"

"No, um, I really have to get home. My parents will be waiting for me," Paul lied. It was the only excuse he could think of.

Looking at his passenger with a mixture of disappointment and anger, the driver removed his chubby hand from Paul's leg and quickly pulled over to the side of the road. Paul got out as quickly as he had got in. The driver sped away.

* * * * *

Paul never went back to Selma Avenue. His prostitution days ended before they began. He avoided the street on his way to work and moved from Hollywood about a month later. He lived in various cities during his life, going from bank job to bank job, but never became part of the "city of night" that he clamoured for in his youth. He decided that security was more important than excitement and eventually ended up working for a small investment firm in San José. He retired last year.

Sometimes, on the weekends, Paul would visit the gay scene in San Francisco, but was mostly ignored by the other men at the bars who seemed to get younger with each visit. Driving home alone, he would comfort himself with the thought that he, at least, had a good pension and a paid-up mortgage.

Paul's hopes and dreams had mostly been replaced by memories of the past; more of his life was behind him than in front of him. And, of course, he was no longer the twink he used to be. His cardiologist was constantly telling him to lose weight. He reassured himself that he had no regrets about his life but sometimes he caught a glimpse of his reflection in a shop window and wondered who the balding, overweight, old man was staring back at him. During those brief moments, he couldn't help but wonder how different, how much more exciting his life might have been, if he had only had the courage to return to Selma Avenue when he was young.

[end]

Nick

I don't remember when I first met Nick, but it must have been at a Narcotics Anonymous meeting – probably at the gay meeting that met on Portobello Road on Tuesday nights – the one I used to see an ageing pop star at until everything he "shared" started appearing in the press. Although the official slogan was "gossip kills" and "who you see here, what you hear here, let it stay here," as soon as word spread that someone famous was going to a particular meeting, the room wasn't big enough to hold all the addicts who were suddenly desperate for recovery.

An addiction to heroin was what brought me to the "fellowship." I was from the States originally and had started using there - first in San Francisco and then New York. I had moved to London thinking that it would be easier to quit in a foreign city. It was what they called doing a "geographical" in the rooms. I didn't know then that it didn't matter where you were. The problem was "you," not the place where you lived.

Nick's addiction had more to do with party drugs and alcohol. He went to gay Alcoholics Anonymous too, but preferred NA to AA; he wasn't exclusively gay, but neither was the gay meeting. Nobody was supposed to be considered "special" or "different" in either "fellowship;" a gay addict was as much an addict as a straight addict, a transgender addict or a bisexual one. Nick was bisexual.

I'd been thinking a lot about him while I recovered at home from a series of heart attacks I had just after my 60th birthday. The heart attacks led to a cardiac arrest which led to general organ failure and a two month medically induced coma. They had tried to insert stents but there was no blood reflow. I even died at one point - but only for a few minutes. After four months, I was finally allowed to go home. Physiotherapists visited daily to get me walking again.

With so much time on my hands I retreated into the past. I found a large box of photographs from my pre-digital past which included one of Nick. There he was, his clear green eyes wide open, seemingly astonished by the camera's flash, as I leaned across his lap to make sure I was included in the shot. I was surprised by how attractive he was – it must have been taken in the early 1990s when my gay friends and I were wearing tight Levis, tight t-shirts and short cropped hair.

Nick looked a lot 'straighter' in the photo - more suburban. He was wearing a sensible two-tone parka, a loose t-shirt with the name of a band I didn't recognise, and his medium brown hair wasn't styled in any particular fashion, as long as it stayed out of his eyes. He wasn't trying to be a type; he was just being "Nick." It was probably his lack of style that made him attractive.

His main claim to fame was that he had climbed the highest mountain in the U.K. – Ben Nevis – when he had AIDS. I had never heard of Ben Nevis before, I only realised what a big deal it was when the priest mentioned it at his funeral as though it was the main accomplishment of his life. For me, the main accomplishment of his life was him. He didn't need any other accomplishments than that.

A couple of months after we met, Nick asked me to become his sponsor in NA – someone who is supposed to guide you through the "12 steps" of recovery. I was an unlikely candidate for a sponsor because I mostly went to meetings to complain about having to go to meetings - or "brainwashing sessions" - as I usually referred to them. One 70-year-old woman with centuries of "clean time" came up to me after one of my "shares" and said, "maybe brainwashing isn't such a bad thing, maybe all our brains could use some washing," like she was talking about a pair of dirty socks. A month later, she arrived at the gay meeting in tears because she had relapsed. She had bought some paracetamol at Boots that contained codeine and then went to a different Boots the next day and bought some more. After that, she spent most of her day hitting up different Boots for the over-the-counter medicine so she wouldn't seem suspicious. She wasn't gay but she was a regular at the gay meeting. She said she liked going there because it was one of the few meetings where people talked so openly about sex.

I agreed to Nick's request, of course. I became his sponsor. Later, he told me it was *because* of my negative attitude that he chose me. He said it would be easier to relapse with me as a sponsor. He was right. We started using together about a month later, but nothing too heavy – just spliff and booze and ecstasy and maybe a line of coke now and then. We stopped going to meetings, of course, and usually just hung around my flat getting out of it and watching videos. Sometimes we'd take a shower together. I don't remember how it started, but it was his idea. We'd get undressed, jump into the shower, and put our arms around each other while the water flowed over us. Neither of us were aroused – we were just two friends taking a shower together. It sounds strange writing about it now but at the time it felt like the most natural thing in the world.

Maybe one of the reasons we never had sex was that he was afraid of giving me the virus; they hadn't discovered combination therapy yet and he knew I wasn't positive. Sometimes he'd be stuck in the hospital with full-blown AIDS, but I never saw him then because he didn't want his friends to see how ill he really was. I could understand that because I had other friends who were "blessed" – the way gay guys referred to other guys with HIV - and saw how quickly they deteriorated from good-looking young guys to gaunt old men with skin so thin that you could almost see through it. Nick would never have wanted me to see him like that.

Besides, he always recovered pretty quickly and then we'd carry on as usual – smoking and drinking and taking downers – he could get almost anything he wanted from his doctors; they knew that the writing was on the wall for AIDS patients and did whatever they could to make their journey as comfortable as possible. I'm an atheist, but God bless the doctors who put their morality aside and helped their patients make it through those days, particularly the ones who helped them end their lives peacefully when the time came for it.

Poor Nick. If he had only managed to hold on a few more years, he would have been able to access the new drugs that turned HIV from a death sentence to a treatable illness. He might have survived. I remember the last time I spoke to him. He rang me from a telephone at the bottom of the steps leading to his room in a hospice. He was in pain and couldn't make it up the stairs. Regardless of what the hospice did, they couldn't get rid of the pain.

"I don't know what to do," he said from the bottom of the stairs. "I'm so tired of all of this. I can't do it anymore. What should I do, Gary?"

We had always been truthful to each other, and I couldn't bring myself to give him false hope now. He was in a hospice. He was dying. We both knew it.

"Nick, it's okay to give up. Maybe it's time."

I don't remember the conversation after that. I was crying but I didn't want him to hear me so I held my hand over the phone, but I was sure that he could still hear the echo of my tears.

* * *

My recovery from the heart attacks seemed to go on forever. Before I got ill, I went to the same café every morning across the street from where I lived for a coffee and croissant. It was the first place I headed when I could finally walk again, eager to visit the staff that I had got to know so well before the hospital.

Except they weren't there anymore. The café hadn't changed but the staff had. Nobody knew who I was, and I didn't know who they were. I'd never seen the tall blonde barista who served me this time. Or had I? There was something familiar about him, but he wasn't from the old staff. I told him how I wanted my coffee – a double macchiato with extra foam on top - and started to explain why having the almost solid layer of foam resting on top of the liquid was so important until I realised that I was sounding like a coffee advert.

"Sorry, I've been stuck inside for such a long time I forgot how to converse."

He laughed at the doddering old man with his NHS walking stick that he saw in front of him. I thanked him and sat at my usual table, next to a window that looked out on the neighbouring alley. They were playing R&B music from the mid-1990s through the café sound system - artists I used to listen to when I was younger like Mary K. Blige and The Braxtons. I suddenly remembered who the barista reminded me of; he looked exactly like Alan, my boyfriend during the '90s – tall, short blonde hair, blue eyes.

I lived in the same flat then that I do now – a Council flat on a side street off Oxford Street near the record shop HMV which has since disappeared. Alan would come over at the end of the week so we could check out the new releases which always came out on a Friday. The romance didn't last very long but our friendship did and so did the visits to HMV. Often friends would come along, and we'd hit Soho afterwards. After the record store, we would usually go to Compton's on Old Compton Street and then to Russell Square for some late-night cruising. Whoever was left ended up spending the night on one of my puffy white sofas that doubled as beds – the perfect place to watch the moon drifting past the tall Centre Point building that you could see from the glass patio doors that led to my balcony. Most Londoners hated Centre Point, but I liked it because its name was lit up in neon – like the pictures of buildings you'd see of Japan or New York. Living in the West End of London was like living in the centre of the world.

Listening to the music in the café, I started to miss the 'good old days' as I looked at my ageing reflection in the window. Strangely, the tinted window appeared to have smoothed out the lines on my face and I looked more like I had in the '90s when I hung out with Alan. Maybe staying indoors, away from the sun, had improved my skin. When I got home, however, I realised it was an illusion; I passed the mirror in the entrance hallway and saw that I looked as old as ever.

The next morning, I decided to go someplace else for coffee - I wanted to avoid the Alan look-a-like - I wanted to avoid the past. Even though I knew yesterday's barista couldn't possibly have been Alan, it was like small pieces of the past had become lodged in my brain and I couldn't get rid of them.

But despite my decision to go elsewhere, I again ended up at my usual café – as if my body had a mind of its own. Someone other than the Alan look-a-like was at the front counter initially but as the new person was making my coffee, Alan appeared through a door next to the espresso machine, carrying a box of paper cups. He saw me, set down his package and smiled: "Good morning, Gary."

I couldn't help asking how he knew my name. He didn't say anything, he just closed one of his hands with the other, like he was doing a magic trick, and then reopened his closed fist. It reminded me of when I was a kid and my parents bought me a magic kit for Christmas.

I expected a miracle from the barista – maybe the appearance of a coin or a dove - but instead he just pointed downwards with a finger of the newly opened hand to the card reader on the counter. He had remembered my name from my debit card during yesterday's transaction.

I smiled at his joke and mumbled something about how it was nice to be remembered, but he was already serving another customer by then and I figured that 'name remembrance' was probably part of his customer service training. He greeted the next customer by his name as well.

I sat down at my usual table. They were playing punk music that day. Punk. Did anyone listen to punk anymore? It was a band I knew from my San Francisco days – the late 1970s when I used to go to a club called the Mabuhay – the period of my life when I first started using the hard drugs that eventually led me to the NA meeting in London where I met Nick.

Did you ever have a feeling that someone was staring

at the back of your head? It felt like that in the café on that day. I turned sideways – there was a banquette against the wall and a long mirror behind it. Maybe it was my own reflection that I felt so strongly, but when I turned and looked at myself in the banquette mirror, I wasn't old anymore. I was as young as I had been in the 1970s.

That's when I saw Sally. She was sitting on the end of the banquette. I lived with her in San Francisco in 1978 in a cockroach-infested flat off Polk Street. She looked just like she had then – like a punk version of Sophia Loren in a black and white photograph. Her dyed black hair was tousled like she had just passed by a wind machine. Her red lips were as dark as she could get them before reaching black and her eyelashes were so thick that it looked like she used house-paint for mascara. She was wearing what she usually wore in the '70s – a man's white dress shirt, the bottom left untucked over a pair of tight black jeans that stopped short of the top strap of her shiny black stilettos.

In the '70s Sally would sit for ages in a dilapidated fake-green leather recliner in our one room dive, separating her eyelashes with an open safety pin while looking at her reflection in a broken piece of mirror she held in her other hand.

I would lay on a mattress on the floor while she was doing her eyes, reading the latest issue of *Punk Globe*.

Sometimes friends would show up at the flat with a cassette they had secretly recorded at a gig the night before on a ghetto blaster they had stolen from the thrift shop down the road. It was one of the happiest times of my life.

Both Sally and I were addicted to heroin and part of our day was devoted to making sure we had enough money to score before withdrawals set in. We'd steal books from shops that sold new books and sell them to shops that sold second-hand books. It was amazing how many books you could fit in the waist of your jeans, covered by the folds of your black trench coat which punks always wore regardless of the weather.

The Sally look-a-like at the café smiled when she saw me – a subtle Mona Lisa smile that I recognised from the past. I turned away. It didn't make sense. It wasn't just that the Sally on the banquette was as young as she was during the 1970s, I knew she was dead. I was still living with her when she died. I never learned exactly what happened, but she had got pregnant by someone in a band who played the Mabuhay and something went wrong while she was waiting for her abortion appointment to come up. We were in our flat one afternoon and she couldn't stop bleeding. I used some of our dope money to take her to Beth Israel in a taxi. The driver was cursing her for bleeding over the back seat of the cab and I was cursing at him for cursing at her and telling him to hurry up. Afterwards, he apologised and told me to forget about the fare. I asked if he wanted help cleaning his cab, but he said, "no, just take care of your friend."

Everything was so confusing at the time. It happened so quickly. The hospital staff took her away immediately and I was left to wait in the main waiting room of Emergency. When I asked how she was, they said they couldn't tell me anything because I wasn't a relative. They had reached some relatives in San Jose who were on their way. A few minutes later they returned and said that the relatives didn't know who I was; that I should leave my details and they would be in touch.

I was starting to get dope sick. I had to get to the book shops to get some money to score. I wanted to have some dope waiting for Sally when she got home later that day. But she never came home. I called the hospital, but they wouldn't give me any information. I left a message for the relatives but the only thing I got back was an eviction notice. Sally's parents owned our flat. I was so angry I wrote back, "What the FUCK has happened to Sally?"

I never got a response. I moved out of the flat and stayed with friends. I heard she was dead through street gossip – I don't remember when. There was no memorial, no good-bye drinks, no songs dedicated to her at the Mabuhay. Suddenly, she just wasn't there anymore. But here she was, now, on the banquette, staring at me. Was it my imagination or did she mouth the words "Hi"?

I left the café. I never wanted to go back there again.

When I got home, I looked in the hallway mirror and I was old again. There had been no Sally at the café. It was just someone who looked like her. Whoever it was probably said "hi," if she did say "hi," because she saw me staring at her.

The next morning, determined to try someplace else, I ended up at the same café as before. I even saw the Alan look-a-like again. I sat at my usual table, listening to the '90s indie style music they were playing. At least it wasn't punk. Maybe the spell had been broken. The music meant nothing to me. I caught a glimpse of myself in the window, but it was a sunny morning, and I couldn't see much of a reflection, so I turned to look at the long mirror on the other side of the room – the one behind the banquette. I squinted my eyes. I was young again. What was going on? I noticed someone sitting at the end of the banquette – a young man this time, not Sally. I squinted again and saw Nick staring back at me.

There was no use trying to explain the image away as a figment of my imagination. The person didn't just look like Nick, he felt like Nick. Not Nick as he would have been now but Nick as he was back then. I was back in the 1990s. Nick was into indie music, especially the

Verve and the Primitive Radio Gods.

The Nick on the banquette saw me looking at him and smiled with those bright green eyes that I remembered so well and that now filled me with such joy and sadness. He motioned for me to sit next to him which I did.

"Long time." he said, staring straight ahead and barely moving his mouth.

I nodded but couldn't think of what to say. How do you start up a conversation with someone who has been dead for more than two decades?

Nick asked if I lived in the same place as before and suggested that we go back to mine for some privacy. We left through the back door of the cafe, walked silently across the courtyard, and entered my building. Inside the flat, I sat in my usual armchair, and he sat on the sofa opposite me.

* * *

"My god, Nick, I don't know what he is going on, but it's so good to see you," I said. "I was so upset when you died. I felt responsible in some way. I told you to die. I didn't even visit you in the hospice."

"I didn't want you to," he said. "I was too ill. You were right. It was my time to go. Don't worry about it. Seriously."

He paused, and then asked, "Got any spliff?"

I laughed. It was definitely Nick.

"I don't smoke anymore, Nick. I can't. I had a bunch of heart attacks a few months ago. I can't even smoke tobacco. Or drink. Or do anything else that's fun."

"What a drag. Hey, do you want to take a shower together like we used to?"

"Sure. Why not?"

We got undressed and walked into the bathroom, passing the mirror above the sink. I couldn't see Nick's image at all – just mine, and I wasn't young anymore.

We turned the shower on, embraced each other, and let the water glide over us. I started crying. Sometimes you don't realise how much you miss someone or something until you experience them again. God, I wished Nick was still around. But he *was* still around. We had our arms around each other. We were hugging each other like in the old days; his arms were as comforting as always, but my grasp was becoming weaker, his body thinner. I couldn't keep hold of him. It was like holding onto a skeleton.

"Nick, are you okay?" I asked.

His bones started to break away in my arms and dissolve into powder. It was like trying to hold onto dust, and then the dust disappeared.

My heart started beating rapidly. Too rapidly. It was missing beats. I had to calm myself down before I had another heart attack. I quickly got out of the shower, grabbed a large bath towel, and went into the front room. Wrapping the towel around myself, I sat in my usual armchair shivering, like an old man. I *was* an old man.

I wondered if I should go back to the bathroom. How could it have been Nick? Or Sally for that matter – or Alan? But I knew it was. I knew it was all of them. I could feel it. Maybe they weren't saying hello, maybe they were saying good-bye.

It was as if my past was dying in front of me but so was my future. When I was young, it always felt like something exciting was around the next corner, but I hadn't had that feeling for such a long time. Sixty-year-olds with a heart condition don't search out exciting times. They avoid them.

It was getting cold. I had left the balcony window partially opened when I went out for the coffee and forgot to close it when Nick and I returned. The afternoon sun was still shining brightly but a cold wind had started to blow through the room which now felt so empty. I wrapped myself up in my large bath towel to keep warm and closed my eyes.

* * *

"Another one..." the ambulance driver observed as he

and his colleague lifted the body onto the stretcher. "This is my third death this week."

"What do you think happened?" his partner asked.

"Who knows? Maybe pneumonia. These old men, they nod off with the window open and don't even realise they're dying."

"But how could they not know they're dying?" his partner asked. "I wonder what goes through their heads."

"All sorts of things, probably. When my nan died, she thought she was talking to Tony Hancock," the driver said.

"Who's Tony Hancock?"

"Some old comedy geezer."

They managed to get the body onto a stretcher and into the lift by tilting it upwards. The neighbour who had reported the smell of "rotting flesh" had already been told to return to her flat.

They loaded the body into the back of the ambulance and the driver started the engine.

"Fancy some lunch after this?" he asked his colleague. "I could do with a pint."

[end]

Blanche

Blanche bought a lottery ticket even though she knew she would be dead by the time the winning numbers were announced that night. It didn't matter. If she won, she could always leave the money to her alcoholic mother and the overactive 12-year-old son she had deserted when she left Arizona to become a punk in San Francisco. She had read about the San Francisco scene in a punkzine called *Punk Globe* that she bought at Jack's, the only record shop in Phoenix that sold punk stuff. Once she found a 45 at Jack's of Patti Smith singing *Piss Factory* with her name spelled wrong. "That'll be worth something someday," a friend told her.

Everyone looked like they were having such a good time in the magazine - young people dancing on top of each other and cute guys in black jeans sneering at the photographer's camera. It didn't matter that they were about twenty years younger than Blanche. She still felt like she had more in common with them than with the housewives of Phoenix.

One morning, while her kid was in school and her mother was sleeping off a hangover, she got up and left - ran away from home at the age of 40. She had "had enough," she wrote in a good-bye letter and said she would contact them once she got settled - except she never got settled - she was too busy getting high.

Now, two years later, she was sitting on the edge of a sheet-less mattress in a welfare hotel at the end of Polk Street writing another note - this time it was a suicide note. It wasn't so much that she regretted moving to San Francisco, she regretted life in general. It wasn't her fault that she was born.

She read and re-read the suicide note, making sure she had got everything right:

> To Whom It May Concern:
>
> I am not writing this to anyone in particular because it will probably be read by a lot of people. All I want is for everyone to know that I love my family and most of my friends and that nobody should feel guilty for what I am about to do. I'm just not that crazy about living anymore. I guess things would be different if I was rich or famous or something, but I'm not, and never will be. A human being can't live without hope. I don't wake up thinking that something exciting might happen today, I wake up wondering how I'm going to get through another day. So, I might as well call it quits now. I had my

chance, and I blew it and it's too late to start all over. Maybe I never had a chance in the first place. Some people are born lucky. I'm not one of them.
Farewell to everyone!

Love, Blanche

She felt like she had left something out, or like she needed to correct something, but she didn't want to overdo it. She was off her head on meth and wanted to make sure that the letter made sense.

She had run into the guy who sold her the meth - Robbie - on Polk Street. He asked her if she wanted a shot.

"Don't worry, it's on me," he said as he stuck the needle into her arm and got a vein on the first hit: "Bingo," he said as the blood swirled up into the syringe.

She was glad that he did it because she could never find a vein when she did it herself. Then he gave her a 'lude for later. She loved Robbie. Why were gay guys always so nice? Straight guys treated her like shit.

She resisted the temptation to add to the note and folded it into an envelope with the lottery ticket she bought earlier. She put the envelope into the zipped section of her purse where she had also put the 'lude.

She didn't want to lose either while she waited for night to fall so that she could take a walk into the sea without anyone noticing.

That damn sunlight! Her thoughts were racing from neurone to neurone. That stuff was strong. What time was it anyway?

She had packed most of her other belongings - clothes that she would never wear again, make-up that would go unused and her most prized possession - her collection of flyers from all the punk gigs she had gone to - in a black trash bag.

She loved those flyers. She wished she could leave them with somebody. She looked through them before she put them in the bag, trying to figure out what the first gig was that she went to or what had caused some of the stains - wasn't that red stain from the time that Ricky Sleeper spilled a bottle of red wine on the flyer? Was that before or after he joined Negative Trend? The Dead Kennedys were probably her favourite band. Or the Avengers.

She put the flyers back in the bag and dragged it down the stairs. What was she waiting for? She might as well leave now. On the way to the lobby, she passed the landlady sitting at the front desk - a large black transvestite who turned tricks at night outside the hotel - giving cheap blow jobs to teenagers in cars who would shout names at her through the car window afterwards.

She didn't particularly like Blanche - she was too near her own age - and she was white and a real woman.

As Blanche went out the door the landlady mumbled, "Good riddance to bad rubbish." Blanche sneered. The landlady knew there was no chance in hell of getting the 2 weeks of rent owed to the hotel. What could she do? Call the cops? The cops were for 'normal' people.

Outside, the sun beat down on Blanche's thinning bleached blonde hair. It felt like a drill going through the top of her head. She needed to waste some time until nightfall. Maybe she should visit some friends from the punk scene and say good-bye, but they might get suspicious and start to ask questions.

Her plan was to walk to the end of Polk Street where there was a small section of sand to the left of Fisherman's Wharf where nobody went because it was mostly mud. But there was a bench there and further out was the sea. She could sit on the bench until it got dark, maybe leave her suicide note there, and then as soon as night fell, she could walk out into the sea. But she couldn't go to the bench now - it was too early. If she sat on it for too long, the cops might notice. What time was it anyway?

"Blanche!"

"Sally!"

Blanche and Sally had lived together in a flat on Post Street when Blanche first moved to San Francisco. They had met at the Mabuhay. Sally's parents paid the rent on the flat and sent her a small stipend to cover her basic expenses until next month's cheque. They figured that she was going through a "phase" and that she would settle down eventually. They didn't understand the punk thing, but it could be worse. At least she hadn't moved to New York. They lived in Paolo Alto - not far - where Sally had been raised. They knew she drank even though she wasn't 21 but would be shocked to find out that she was a junkie whose boyfriend was a dealer called Mitchell who had links to organised crime and a ready supply of dope.

"What are you doing?" Sally asked. "What's in that trash bag?"

"I don't know. Stuff. I'm going back home to take care of my kid."

"What kind of stuff?" Sally asked. Blanche looked like a bag lady. "Where are you living now?"

"Nowhere. I told you I'm going home," she said, half-hoping that Sally would ask her to move in with her until she got on her feet.

"Is that your luggage?" Sally asked, pointing at the trash bag again, and laughing.

"Yes. It's all I had. It's my clothes and all my flyers - hey Sally do you want my flyers - I saved them from the Mabuhay and all the punk gigs. It's kind of like a history of my life." Blanche opened her bag and took out a handful of flyers. Her eyes were like two black poker chips.

"Are you out of it?" Sally asked.

"Don't you want the flyers? It would be something to remember me by."

"Fuck the flyers. What are you on?"

"Meth. Robbie had some meth."

Sally's mind worked quickly. If Blanche was that high, maybe she was ready to come down. "I could probably get something from Mitchell for if you want to come down from the meth."

"I don't have any money. Just the bus ticket and about five dollars for food on the way."

"Maybe Jerry and Janie would split a bag with you. It's really good right now."

Sally knew that if she could sell Blanche a twenty-dollar bag, she could take about a quarter of it before she passed it on, and her morning hit would be taken care of. Jerry and Janie were two friends - they looked like twin sisters - who lived on Bush and earned their money by turning tricks in Union Square. Sally and Blanche knew them from the Mabuhay.

"No, no I'm fine. Robbie gave me a quaalude to come down." Blanche said.

Jerry and Janie would probably still be asleep anyway. Oh well, she could do Mitchell's cotton. He always left a good cotton for Sally in the morning and some dried-up dope in the spoon. All she had to do was add water. It wasn't as much as she could pilfer from Blanche, but at least it would get rid of the sniffles and the other aches and pains of withdrawal.

She imagined the cotton sitting there in the spoon, waiting for her. Sally was the only person who knew which welfare hotel Mitchell lived in. Somewhere in Nob Hill. When he said he lived in Nob Hill his customers imagined an expensive flat, paid for from all the money he made from selling dope, but it was just a crappy run-down room like everyone else had. He shot up his profits.

"Well, I'm sure you'll be back soon," Sally said. "My phone's been turned off but if you ever do come back just buzz my flat - you know the code - one quick one and then two longer ones."

"Okay. Thanks Sally. I was thinking. Maybe..."

Sally knew what she was going to ask, and the answer was no. The last thing she wanted was a bag lady staying at her place. Blanche had trouble written all over her. Sally cut her off before she could finish her question: "I'm really sorry Blanche but I've gotta go. I told Mitchell I'd be at his place five minutes ago. I'm already late." She crossed the street and headed toward Nob Hill.

Love you, Sal!" Blanche shouted after her. Sally waved her hand without turning around.

Blanche stood on the curb with her black plastic trash bag. What was she going to do now? It was too sunny to kill herself. Why had she even bothered to pack her things away? It was mostly because of the flyers - she couldn't bear to throw away all those flyers. Going to all those gigs - it was the only thing she had accomplished in her life.

She had an idea - maybe Miguel would want the flyers. He was making a student film about the punks. That's how Blanche had met him - at a Mutants gig at the Art Institute. She had followed him and his Bolex around one night as he interviewed the punks, hoping he might film her. But he kept passing her by. Finally, she tapped him on the shoulder and when he turned around, she joked "I'm ready for my close-up" like Gloria Swanson in *Sunset Boulevard*. But he didn't get the joke. He knew she wanted to be interviewed because he noticed her following him earlier, but he wanted to film young punks - people his age. But when she asked, he couldn't say no. It would be like saying no to his mother.

The first question he asked was how old she was, and he could tell by her expression that he had made a horrible mistake. She looked like she was going to start crying. But she didn't cry, and he carried on with the interview and they often ran into each other after that - either on Polk Street or at the Mabuhay. One time she asked how the film was going - was it finished - could she see it? He said it was just a student thing, something for his class, not for the public. He didn't have the heart to tell her that he had cut her footage out.

They became friends anyway. Occasional friends. He didn't do as many drugs as Blanche and her friends - he felt obligated to go to classes and get a degree because of how much it was costing his parents in Spain and, who knows, maybe he would be a famous director someday.

He worked in The Bagel further down on Polk Street, but she couldn't remember what days he worked or what day it was now. If he was there, he was good for a free coffee which would top up the meth. As she walked down Polk, she prayed to a god she didn't believe in: 'Please, dear God, let Miguel be at work, please dear God let him be at work…'

She repeated it over and over even though God had never answered her prayers before. There were so many times she had prayed in the past for the dope to be good on her way to score and it wound up being shit.

"Blanche!"

"Miguel!"

Thank God he was there. She stepped up into the cafe and set her bag down at an empty table.

"What's that?" he asked.

"My stuff," she said. "I'm leaving."

"What do you mean?"

"Going home."

"So suddenly?" He had seen her at the Mabuhay - when was it - the night before last? She hadn't mentioned anything then.

"Is something wrong?" he asked.

"No, nothing's wrong. I guess we'll all be going home someday."

"Coffee?"

"Yeah, definitely."

"I'll be sorry to see you go," he said.

"Um, I don't have any money," she said as he started making her coffee.

He laughed. "Since when did you have any money? It's on the house."

He poured her a coffee in a large cup which entitled her to free refills. He brought it to her table and wrote his address and phone number in Spain down on a page from his orders pad.

"Here, this is my family home in Valencia. They will always know where I am. Maybe you can come visit me in Spain."

"Oh, Miguel, I wish I could."

He looked at her. She sounded sad but looked wide-eyed and happy. Then he noticed how large her pupils were which meant she was probably on speed. He went back to his counter to serve some customers who wanted take-aways. Blanche opened her trash bag and started to go through the flyers, spreading them out on the table.

"What are you doing?" he asked from the counter.

"I'm looking for the first flyer – from the first gig I went to. See, these are all the flyers from the punk gigs I went to. I saved them."

"Wow, that's great. What a great thing to have. I wish I had done that."

She reached out, both of her hands filled with flyers. "Here, Miguel, take them. You can have all of them. You probably went to a lot of the same gigs."

The way she held out the flyers - it was like someone in church back in Spain asking forgiveness for their sins. Something was wrong. He should sit with her, he thought, but more customers came in.

"You keep them," he said. "You'll appreciate them later." After a slight pause, he added: "When you're old."

'Who was he kidding?' Blanche thought. She was already old, and he knew it. They all did. She looked at the mess of papers on the table. That's all they were. Meaningless printed papers representing a meaningless life.

"I'm joking!" he said. "You will never get old."

As he made another group of customers their coffees, she stuffed the flyers back into the bag.

'What a stupid idea,' she thought. Why would

anyone want her flyers? It was *her* life, not theirs. When she died, so would her memories. She didn't even feel sad. She felt relieved. She should have left the bag at the hotel.

It started to get dark toward the end of coffee number 3. Time had flown by so quickly. Miguel had been busy most of the time with other customers and she had watched everyone rushing back and forth outside. 'Where was everyone going?' she wondered. 'Why?'

She could feel the meth wearing off but still felt speedy from the coffee. It would be getting dark soon - maybe an hour or so. She decided to walk down to the bench at the end of Polk Street. She could sit for a while and watch the sea until it was completely dark, and then take her walk into the sea. She took the quaalude before she left the cafe to boost her courage. It would take about an hour to work. She usually took two of them to get high, but Robbie's 'ludes were really strong - from Mexico - still, she prayed to God that it would be strong - that she would only need one. But even if it wasn't strong, it would be enough to give her the courage she needed.

* * *

By the time she got to the bench, Blanche was exhausted. Her trash bag had got heavier and heavier.

She should have just put it in one of the large trash bins on Polk Street, but she couldn't bear to do that to her flyers.

She plopped the bag on the bench and took the envelope out of her purse that contained the suicide note and forced it between two slats in the bench so that the wind wouldn't blow it away. Hopefully, a passing stranger would find the note and the bag and, who knows, she might finally make the papers. She'd be famous at last - not for existing but for not existing.

Although the light was fading, it was still too light to go into the sea. The tide had gone out which meant a further walk - more of a risk that she would be seen. She began to feel the warmth of the quaalude going through her body and she was glad that it was working. Feeling groggy, she decided to lay down on the bench for a few minutes - just until darkness fell. She used the trash bag as a pillow.

She was woken up two hours later by a newspaper flapping around her face. Thank God she woke up. She checked to make sure the envelope was still secure in the slats, and it was. It was time to go.

She looked at the dark black sea in front of her and then the city behind her which was coming to life for all the nighttime excitement. She could see the lights of the strip joints on Nob Hill - an oversized Carol Doda swinging in neon above the club where Doda performed. Her breast implants were so heavy that all she could do was sit on a swing onstage and sing off-key. Blanche knew another stripper at the club - a girl named Blondine - who got her in free a couple of times.

She wondered what Sally was doing now. Probably getting stoned with Mitchell in his room in Nob Hill - not far from the strip joint. Some people had all the luck.

She thought about how much she loved the city when she first arrived and how quickly she had fallen in with the Mabuhay crowd. She might have been older than them, but she had one thing in common which automatically gave her entry into the world of outsiders. The desire for drugs. Lots of them.

It was like belonging to a group with the same hobby. If it hadn't been drugs it could have been stamp collecting. The punks accepted her despite her age - or at least pretended to. Everyone was an outsider in that scene, but what happens when you start feeling like you're outside the outsiders? When you just feel alone?

She was surprised by how much the tide had gone out, but it wouldn't be a problem in the dark. She didn't mind walking in mud. She took off her stilettos and put them on the newspaper on the bench. She noticed it was the last edition of today's paper - it must be after 8 pm. She laughed. The winning lottery numbers would be in it. It didn't take her long to find the results. She had played it so many times in the past, always hoping for a win and never getting one. Each time she would say it was the last time she would play - what a fool she had been to buy that last ticket. Why, when she was going to die, anyway?

She read the winning numbers. Something was wrong. She read them again. She panicked. No, it wasn't panic - it just felt like panic. It was something else. Her hands were shaking as she pried the suicide envelope from the slats of the bench and opened it. She looked at the ticket inside. The numbers matched. The numbers matched!

Blanche had won the lottery. The jackpot was three million dollars. Three million! She wanted to scream - to tell someone the good news but there was nobody to tell.

'Fuck em' she thought. Fuck Sally and Mitchell and Jerry and Janie and everyone at the Mabuhay who had treated her like someone to tolerate instead of a friend.

"They can all go to hell." she said to herself, as she put her stilettos on and headed back to the city.

Blanche was suddenly a millionaire. Her problems were solved.

[end]

Made in United States
Troutdale, OR
01/14/2024

16935762R00077